"I'm sorry, Matt. You should go."

Peg rubbed her hands together. Why had she allowed herself to steal private moments with Matt?

"That's ridiculous, Peg. We've done nothing wrong." He stood.

"Please, Matt. You wouldn't understand."

"Try me."

"Please," Peg pleaded. What could she say? This wasn't the way to tell him the truth about herself and her past—in one foolish moment of wanting to be alone with Matthew, she might have ruined twenty years of restoration. How could she have been so foolish?

Matt lifted her chin with his finger and caressed her lips with his thumb. "Since I've already soiled your pristine reputation, then I guess you won't mind this."

He captured her lips with his. Peg found herself looping her arms around his neck. Her whole world crumbled around her feet as tears ran down her cheeks. He released her and boldly stepped away.

"Good day, Miss Martin. If you can't trust me, then we have no relationship."

LYNN A. COLEMAN is a Martha's Vineyard native who now calls the tropics of Miami, Florida, home. She is a minister's wife who writes to the Lord's glory through the various means of articles, short stories, and a web site. She has three grown children and seven grandchildren. She also hosts an inspirational romance writing workshop on the Internet, manages an inspirational romance web site, and serves as president of the American Christian Romance Writers organization. Visit her web page at www.lynncoleman.com.

HEARTSONG PRESENTS

Southern Treasures

Lynn A. Coleman

Heartsong Presents

To my church family. May God continue to bless us as we work together to bring God's love to various cultures and people in Miami, Florida, and beyond. I love you all and thank you for your faithful prayer support.

A note from the author:
I love to hear from my readers! You may correspond with me by writing:

> Lynn A. Coleman
> Author Relations
> PO Box 719
> Uhrichsville, OH 44683

ISBN 1-58660-386-8

SOUTHERN TREASURES

All Scripture quotations, unless noted, are taken from the King James Version of the Bible.

All of the characters and events in this book are fictitious. Any resemblance to actual persons, living or dead, or to actual events is purely coincidental.

Cover design by Nancy White.

PRINTED IN THE U.S.A.

one

Key West, 1868

"Ship's a-comin'!"

Peg heard the bustle of folks outside her storefront window. When a ship came to port, everyone tended to notice. She slid the needle into the white linen cloth and placed it on the counter. Holly leaves and red berries gave the napkin the Christmas flavor she missed. Stretching her back, she stepped up to the bay window overlooking Key West harbor. She loved her little shop and the view.

A two-masted schooner with a black hull and white trim pulled up to the long dock. It still amazed her how shallow the waters were around the island, so unlike the waters around Savannah. Out of habit, she looked toward the stern of the boat to see the name of the vessel and its point of origin. Even after all these years, she still feared running into people she had known back home.

The Patriot, out of Boston, Massachusetts. A smile creased her face. She watched as the men secured the lines, then helped the passengers off the ship. Peg giggled, watching them regain their legs as they waddled down the pier.

Nathaniel Farris bounced down the gangplank from the boat. Peg waved. Nathaniel turned in the direction of Peg's store and also waved. She knew he couldn't see her, but she also knew he was well aware of her practice of watching the ships unload.

5

Ellis Southard marched up the pier, shook hands with Nathaniel, and proceeded to make his way onboard the ship. Peg stepped back from the window. Ellis always made a point to get to know the captains of the various ships. His business depended upon reliable export of his sponges.

"Anyone interesting?"

Peg jumped and turned around to meet her customer, Vivian Matlin. "Good morning, Vivian. How are you today?"

"Fine, fine. Tell me—did anyone interesting arrive? I can't see as far as I used to." The gray haired woman came up close to the counter.

Peg glanced back out the window. A stately man, with dark hair and silver sideburns, braced himself against the piling, allowing his body the time it needed to adjust to solid ground.

"Well, Nathaniel Farris returned from his latest trip."

"He's such a fine jeweler. Can't believe he escorts some of his jewelry to New York, though. You'd think he'd trust someone else to do that."

"Ah, but that's because of a sweet little woman who also lives in New York," Peg confided.

"You don't say," Vivian grinned. "Tell me more."

Peg smiled. She knew more details than the rest of the island residents. Nathaniel had proposed marriage to Julie this trip. He'd made her the most beautiful engagement ring Peg had ever seen. And by the smile on his face Peg could tell that Julie had accepted. "You'll have to ask Nate."

"Oh, it's Nate now. Come on, Peg. First you tell me there's a special woman in New York, now you're calling Nathaniel Farris by a nickname. You're trying to confuse an old woman, aren't you?"

Peg chuckled. "Possibly."

"Oh, phooey. You used to be the best source of island gossip.

What's come over you?" Vivian pushed.

"Conviction, I guess. It finally occurred to me that if I didn't want my secrets talked about on the streets, I shouldn't be talking about others."

"Oh, well, that's a low blow." Vivian smiled. "But you're right. It's hard when it's the island's favorite pastime."

"Yes, I know." Peg went to the counter and pulled a package out from underneath. "Here you go, Vivian."

"I'm so excited. May I open it and see?"

"Of course."

"You do such marvelous work. My granddaughter will be so surprised to get this for Christmas." Vivian delicately lifted the fancy box covered with a printed fabric and lined with lace. The box alone was quite a gift. But Vivian had insisted that, for her first Christmas as a wife, her granddaughter needed to have something very special.

"Oh my, Peg. This is wonderful." Vivian's voice caught in her throat. "Even in my younger days, when my eyes were good and my fingers nimble, I couldn't have done something as lovely as this."

"Trisha deserves it." Peg beamed. She loved when people were genuinely pleased with her work. The store carried crafts from a variety of island residents, but the thrill of a special sale like this—or the linen napkins she had been embroidering earlier for Bea Southard—made her feel useful.

Vivian's blue-veined hands pulled out the lady's blouse Peg had transformed. A fine lace border lined the collar and cuffs. Delicate tea roses traced the tips of the collar, and a small bouquet draped high over the left breast. A ring of tiny tea roses encircled each buttonhole and cufflink. It wasn't Peg's normal fare, which amounted primarily to making napkins and linen tablecloths, but Vivian was a good customer, and she had purchased the blouse. Peg praised the Lord she had been able to fulfill Vivian's desire.

Vivian gently placed the garment back in the box. Her hands shook with emotion. "It's beautiful. Thank you."

"You're welcome. I enjoyed it." And she truly had. The money she would make from the sale wouldn't come close to compensating her for the hours she'd spent on it, but that didn't matter, not really. "Charity begins at home," she recalled her grandmother saying on more than one occasion.

Vivian fished through her drawstring purse. "I can't believe this is only costing me a dollar. You're sure that's enough?"

No, but that's not the point, she reminded herself. "Yes." After all, hadn't Vivian helped her get this business off the ground during the war? Hadn't she been the one to help drum up the local residents to come into the store? Vivian Matlin, advertiser extraordinaire. She was the best advertising Peg's store, Southern Treasures, ever had.

Nathaniel Farris walked in. His broad grin spoke volumes. "Looks like it went well, Nathaniel."

His grin slipped. "In one way, yes, in another, no."

"Oh?"

?a

Matt scanned the tropical island while regaining his land legs. The captain had warned him to expect a certain amount of unsteadiness. The trip from Savannah seemed short enough, but he'd watched the folks struggle down the dock. Pride dictated some decorum. If he were going to establish a business office in Key West, he didn't want the locals' first impression to be that of an unstable man.

Thankfully, he'd convinced Micah to join him during his Christmas break from school. Micah was the real reason he'd come to Key West. Granted, the business would prosper in this strategic location, but Micah's future—and his past—quite possibly rested upon this small remote island.

Matt eased out a pent up breath.

Today is not the day to be dwelling on that, Lord. Lead me to the right location and the right individuals for this business, Matt silently prayed. He lifted his brown derby, wiped the headband with his handkerchief, and placed it back upon his head.

"May I help ya, Sir?" a gangly Negro boy asked with a smile as bright as the sunshine.

"I've rented a room from a Mr. Isaac Salinger. Are you familiar with this man?"

"I know where he lives. Would you like me to show the way?"

The boy was probably trying to earn a coin or two, what with Christmas coming on. Matt was confident he could find the place with the help of the instructions on the letter in his pocket, but he had to smile at the lad's entrepreneurial spirit. "That would be most agreeable. Shall we wait for my luggage?"

"Momma won't worry none if I'm a few minutes late. I can wait."

"What's your name, Lad?"

"Ben. Benjamin Hunte."

"Well, Ben, it's a pleasure to meet you."

The boy nodded and leaned toward him. In a hushed voiced he added, "If you don't mind me saying so, Sir, you need to get in the shade. Dem dark clothes in this heat isn't wise. Unless, of course, you're used to it."

Considering the trickle of sweat running down the back of his neck, he figured the boy made sense. Savannah was hot in the summer, although it cooled down some in the winter.

"You might be right." Matt scanned the shoreline. There were a few palm trees, but not much shade. "Where do you suggest I wait?"

"That cluster of palm trees might help some, but iffin you have a light shirt on under your overcoat, take the coat off."

The lad had a thin cotton shirt with short sleeves and a pair of light cotton trousers hanging loosely on him, with the cuffs rolled up to just below the knees. A pair of sandals adorned his feet. Matt's long jacket, vest, and wool pants contrasted like night and day. Matt removed his jacket and draped it over his arm. "Is this better?"

The boy tossed his head from side to side. "Not much, but you'll get used to it, iffin you're going to be here for awhile."

"I'm hoping to." At least as long as it took to explore the possibility of setting up his business here.

"Hey, Ben. What are you doing down here?" A full-bearded gentlemen in his thirties approached from the ship. Matt had seen him board the ship shortly after it docked.

"Mr. Ellis, I'm helping him—" The boy pointed in his direction. "He needs to find Mr. Salinger's place."

"I see. And does your Momma know you're down here?"

"No, Sir."

"What about Mo?"

"I saw Dad a few minutes ago. He knows." The boy puffed out his chest.

The stranger extended his hand. "Name's Ellis Southard. Ben, here, is the oldest son of my foreman."

That explains the man's familiarity with the child but— "Pleasure to meet you, Mr. Southard." Matt extended his hand and exchanged a short courteous handshake with Ellis Southard. He always believed you could tell a lot about a person by his or her handshake. This one was firm and straight to business. "My name is Matthew Bower. I'm looking into using Key West as a possible location for my export business."

"It's a busy port. What do you export?"

"Cotton. I'm based in Savannah, but the war was hard on my industry."

"On a lot of men's, I'm afraid. I'm not sure how a cotton export would work for you here, but if I can help, just let me know. I deal in sponges. It's a natural product for the area, and the demand for them is growing."

"Interesting. I export from Georgia, as well as the Louisiana and Alabama areas, so it seemed logical to see if Key West would give me an advantage over waiting for the cotton to sail up to Savannah."

"Makes sense." Ellis Southard nodded slightly. "I hate to run, but I'm on a tight schedule. Ben here will show you where to go. See that dock over there?" He pointed to a dock to the left of where they stood. It was long, and loaded with brown and yellow balls, obviously sponges. "That's my dock. Come on over after you're settled in. I can give you a general idea of the time schedule of the ships."

"Thank you. That's very kind of you."

"Just being neighborly." Ellis Southard waved and headed down the dock toward shore.

"Friendly."

"Most folks know everyone here," Ben offered.

Matt hadn't realized he'd spoken out loud. "Appears so. Your father works for Mr. Southard?"

"Mo is my second dad. My father, he died in the war."

"I'm sorry to hear that, Son." And he truly was. He lost a brother to that war. And he'd been fighting his personal politics on the subject ever since.

Finally, his trunk was lowered and brought off the ship by

some seamen. "Can you bring it to the end of the dock?" he asked them.

"For two bits." One sailor cocked a grin.

"One."

The two grumbled and carried the trunk to the end of the dock. He'd need to rent a wagon or something to bring his trunk to Isaac Salinger's.

The boy tugged on his shirtsleeve. "I can get a wheelbarrow."

"Thanks. I think that would be a good idea."

Ben ran off like lightening was licking at his feet. Matt ambled down the dock. The two crewmen walked up to him and held out their palms. He tossed them a silver dollar and figured they could work out splitting it between them. He sat down on his trunk and visually examined the local businesses. The harbor seemed lined with boats and warehouses. Tucked in among them, he noticed a store.

A store? Sure enough, in the heart of a trading port was some sort of ladies' store. He could barely make out the sign. S O U T H, *Southern*, T R E A S, *Treasures*, Southern Treasures? What kind of a business was that?

Matt heard the sound of iron hitting rock and turned to see Ben pushing a wheelbarrow just about as big as himself down the street. Matt rushed over to relieve the boy. "Where'd you get this?"

"Mr. Ellis."

Either Ellis Southard was quite important to Key West, or he was just a very friendly man. On the other hand, Ben's stepfather was the foreman of Ellis Southard's business. "Tell Mr. Ellis I said thank you when you return it for me."

Ben nodded and stood back while Matt lifted his trunk onto the wheelbarrow. "What's that store over there?" he asked the boy.

"Southern Treasures."

"What kind of a store is it?"

"Mostly ladies things. My dad bought my mom some fancy napkins and a tablecloth from there for her as a wedding present."

"Oh. Are there other stores in town?"

"Sure. But Miss Martin, she owns Southern Treasures. She likes being on the water."

"Martin?"

"Yes, Peg Martin."

Peg Martin! Margaret Martin—Lord, it can't be that easy to find this woman, can it?

two

Peg slipped the hard-earned dollar into the cash drawer. In reality it was a tenth, a tithe, of what she should have charged. But a gentle breeze of pleasure calmed her. It was right to do unto others as she would like them to do for her.

When Vivian exited the building, Peg returned her gaze to Nathaniel. "What happened?"

"She turned me down."

"Is that woman out of her mind?" Peg placed her hands on her hips. "Did you show her the ring?"

"Never got a chance." Nathaniel's shoulders slumped.

"Well, you best set yourself right down and tell me what happened. Start from the beginning." Peg settled on a stool behind the counter as Nathaniel sat on a stool opposite her in front of the counter.

"Not much to tell," he said, folding and unfolding his hands. "I came calling, and she seemed distant. Not like any time prior. It was all so strange."

"Did you ask her to marry you?"

"No, not really. I asked her to go out to dinner with me, and she said she was busy."

"That doesn't seem like the woman you described before."

"That's my point. She was different. She avoided my touch. It was all rather bizarre." Nathaniel looked up and caught her eyes. "She wouldn't even look at me."

"Did you speak with her father, mother, anyone?"

"No one was talking. Her father suggested I return home.

Nothing for me in New York."

"Ouch." Peg reached over and placed her hand on top of his. "Nate, something isn't adding up. Pray about it, and write her some letters. See if she starts warming up."

"I don't know, Peg. It seemed so final."

Peg cared for Nate, not in a romantic way, but he was a good and honest man. She wanted to storm up to New York and demand to know what happened. On the other hand, she thought of two possible answers right off. One, the woman had fallen in love with another. Two, she had been violated. Her own past made her sensitive to these kinds of reactions—the family's shame, the woman not wanting to touch or even look at Nathaniel. But she could be all wrong, and she didn't want to pollute Nathaniel's mind with such horrific facts of life. It was probably none of her business, but she would be penning a letter off to Julie Adams as soon as Nathaniel left the store.

"Do you love her, Nate?"

"You know I do."

"Then fight for her. Write to her. Keep writing until you feel nothing for her. Or until the Lord tells you it's hopeless."

"Do you think she'll even read my letters?"

"Maybe not at first, but give her time. Something must have happened." Peg clamped her jaw shut. She wasn't going to say another word.

Nathaniel pulled out the ring. "I was thinking of giving this to my best friend."

Peg stared at the small jewel case.

"On the trip home. I did a lot of thinking." He rolled the box between his long, slender fingers. "You and I get along so well, I was—"

"No," Peg said with a bit too much force. Nate jumped and

blinked. "Sorry. I like you Nate but not as a woman should love a man she marries."

"Yes, I feel the same way about you. You're more like my older sister."

"Older, huh? Thanks."

Nate chuckled. "Sorry."

It was true, though: She was getting on in years. At thirty-eight, she was an old maid, but she wanted it that way. It was her destined lot, her payment for her past mistakes. "Now you know it's not polite to tease a woman about her age."

"I was going to say, before you interrupted me," he winked, "that, unlike Mo and Lizzy, I don't see us getting married as friends. I was just feeling low."

"And this is to make me feel better—picking on my age?" Peg teased.

Nate fumbled for his words. "Oh. . .I mean. . .well. . .oh, just pull the conch out of my mouth. Maybe I'm not designed for romancing a woman."

Peg chuckled. "Your approach could use some work."

She glanced back at the ship. Most of the passengers were off. The distinguished looking gentleman had taken off his jacket and was talking with Benjamin Hunte. "Did you mingle with the passengers?" she asked Nathaniel.

"Some, why do you ask?"

"Just curious. Who's that man speaking with Ben Hunte?"

He glanced out the window. "That's Matt Bower, a businessman from Savannah."

"Savannah?" Peg felt the room sway. She took in a deep breath, eased it out slowly, closed her eyes, and sucked in another breath.

Calm yourself, she chided herself. *There've been others from Savannah.* Never, not even once in the twenty years she'd been on Key West, had anyone ever addressed her past. Of course, she kept a low profile. Most folks didn't even know she came from Savannah. Not that she kept it a secret, but she didn't go reminding everyone every time she turned around either.

She opened her eyes and focused on the two blurred images of Nathaniel in front of her. His hands were now holding hers. "Are you all right?"

"Fine, must be the heat." She pulled her right hand from his grasp and fanned herself to hide her duplicity. *Get a grip,* she reprimanded herself. *It's been twenty years.*

"Shall I get you some iced tea or something?"

"I'm fine. I have some water in the back room. If you'll excuse me, I'll go fetch some."

"Sure, I need to get to my store anyway." Nathaniel slipped off his stool. "Peg?"

She turned and faced him.

"Thanks. I appreciate your friendship."

"You're welcome. I'm sure it will work out." She smiled. At least, she hoped she was smiling.

In the back room, a narrow storage space that followed the backside of the building, she chipped some ice from the icebox and poured herself a glass a water. "Lord, I know I should be over this, please give me strength."

"Hello? Anyone in here?" a male voice called out from the storefront.

Peg straightened her skirt and exited the back room. "May I help—" Her voice caught. Her throat constricted.

Sweat beaded on her forehead.

Her hands turned to ice.

The room darkened.

Prickles traveled up her skin as the past slammed into the present.

The room spun.

Darkness. . .escape. . .

❧

Matt caught the delicate blond in his arms before her head hit the floor. *Does she know who I am, Lord? How could she?* he wondered. He pulled a decorative pillow down from the shelves and placed it under her head.

"What happened to Miss Martin?" Ben leaned over her.

"Not sure. Do you have a doctor on the island?"

Ben nodded.

"Would you please go get him?"

"Be right back." Ben ran from the store.

Matt released her and folded her arms across her belly. He eyed a small pitcher in the back room she'd just exited. Had the heat overtaken her? It was warm, but it didn't seem that hot. And if she lived here all the time, why would this moderate heat bother her?

He fetched the pitcher and a small towel that hung on a post beside the ice box.

Ice box. He opened it, chipped off some ice, and wrapped it in the towel.

Beside her again, he gently dabbed her face with the cool cloth. *Father, she's beautiful. Of course, she would be.*

She groaned.

Her eyes fluttered open and closed.

Blue, of course.

"Hello." He waited.

Her eyes darted back and forth.

"You fainted. Here drink some of this." Matt lifted her head and placed the glass to her soft pink lips.

Her gaze focused. "Who are you?"

"Matthew Bower. But most folks just call me Matt."

"Do I know you?"

"No, Miss Martin, we just met."

She took another sip. "I'm sorry. I don't know what came over me."

"Doc Hansen is on his way," Ben huffed from the doorway.

"Thank you, Ben."

"You're welcome, Sir."

Ben sat beside Peg Martin, who was now sitting on the floor. Matt realized he was still holding her head for support.

"Are you all right, Miss Martin?" Ben asked.

"I'll be fine, Ben. Thanks."

"Ain't nothing. Just came in to show Mr. Bower your store."

She looked into Matt's eyes again, seeking an answer to her unanswered question. *No, you don't know me,* he realized, *but I certainly know you and all about your past.* He glanced down to her ring finger. Her hands were slender and lightly bronzed from living on this island. But her ring finger was empty, and she was still going by her maiden name. Could she be the one? How many Margaret Martins could there be on such a small island? "The boy said you sold fine linens in here."

"You're looking for linens?" She knitted her eyebrows.

She'd caught him at his deception. "Truth be told, Ma'am, I was simply admiring a storefront in the middle of an export harbor. I, myself, am in the export business."

"I see."

"Peg?" a voice from behind queried. Doc Hansen, Matt presumed. "Ben said you fell."

"Mr. Bower says I fainted."

"Did you eat this morning?" The doctor began his examination. Matt got up and turned his back to give her privacy. There was no question in his mind; she was the one. The one he'd been searching for since he learned the truth. *The truth. . . God help me, I don't know if I can do it, Lord. I certainly just can't—*

"Dr. Hansen, I'm staying at Isaac Salinger's place. If you'll be needing anything from me, I'll be there." Without turning around, he added, "I hope you're feeling better, Miss Martin. Good day."

Matt flew out of the store faster than a goose flying south for the winter. Whatever possessed him to go into that store the first moment he came into town?

He kicked a sun-bleached hunk of coral out of his path. Picking up the ends of the wheel barrel, he said to Ben, "Suppose you show me where Mr. Isaac Salinger lives before anyone else passes out from this heat."

"I never known Miss Martin to faint like that. She's been here forever."

Matt stole a glance back at Southern Treasures. It was a quaint store, he had to admit. Seemed to fit her delicate beauty. He wasn't a connoisseur of fancy lady things, but he'd bought Esther a few niceties in his day.

Esther. What would she say if she knew? Would she bury the secret like Dr. Baker had? Or would she be as compelled as he had been to find Margaret Martin and tell her the truth?

Matt raked his hand through his damp hair. It *was* hot today. Perhaps Miss Martin was simply stricken by the heat after all.

No, there was a look in her eyes when he walked in the store. As if she knew—but how could she?

three

"Three weeks," Peg mumbled and went back to her work. It had been three weeks since she'd made a perfect fool of herself fainting in front of Matthew Bower. The man seemed perfectly harmless, but she still couldn't face him. If she saw him coming down the street, she'd hurry off in another direction just to avoid him. Daniel, her brother, had even had some business with Matt. He seemed normal enough, yet there was something about him that unnerved her. The worst part was that she couldn't figure out why.

Peg stitched the final blue heron on the baby blanket for Bea and Ellis Southard's boy. He looked just like his father with his brown hair and blue-gray eyes. Southard eyes, Peg decided. Their nephew, Richie, had the same blue-gray eyes. The same shade of blue she'd used to embroider the heron.

The bell over the door jingled. Peg looked up with a smile, then dropped it immediately. Her hands gripped the blanket.

"Good morning, Miss Martin." Matthew Bower stood tall with his handsome jet-black hair and green eyes. The silver streaks on his sideburns made him look even more refined, if that were possible.

Peg swallowed. "Good morning, Mr. Bower. How may I help you?"

"You can tell me how you are. I've been concerned, but every time I've seen you in town you've run in the opposite direction."

He'd seen her. Heat assaulted her cheeks as strong as the

hot sun at noon bore down on the small tropical isle. "I'm sorry. I'm rather embarrassed by my behavior the other day."

"For pity sakes, Ma'am, whatever for? You simply fell victim to this heat. I'm still adjusting to it. I certainly understand why things slow down in the middle of the day and don't really resume until midafternoon." He stepped closer to the counter. "I met your brother, Daniel. Nice fella. Pretty wife, too."

"Carmen, she's a sweetheart. Perfect wife for Daniel."

"So it seems." He surveyed the various shelves of the store. "I haven't been in here since I first arrived. If you don't mind, I'd like to browse."

"Help yourself. You'll find we have a variety of items. Several island folks make them, and I sell them."

"Your brother seems to think rather highly of your skills." Matthew's hand traced the stitching she'd done on a place-mat. Did he know what work was hers? How could he? *Lord, what is going on with me?*

"Your brother says you also hail from Savannah. That's where I'm from."

"Yes," she croaked out. Did he know her shame? Did he know Billy? *And why did Daniel open his big mouth? Okay, Daniel doesn't usually have a big mouth, but this time. . .*

"I'm looking into Key West as a port for my exporting business. I distribute cotton to South America and Europe."

Why is he giving me all this information?

"Savannah's a good harbor, but I'm not the only distributor there. I'm looking to expand my business and speed up the delivery time by working from here."

"We certainly have enough boats passing through," Peg said lamely. What else could she say? She didn't know why the man was here; she couldn't help her attraction to him, and yet she was terrified by him. All of which were silly reasons.

After all, she was a grown woman, completely in control of her life and her destiny. She was right with God, and she'd made her peace with the past. She had a good life. So why was Matthew Bower so unsettling?

"That's what attracts me to Key West." Matthew stepped further away, examining the next shelf over. In front of him stood items carved from coral rock. He lifted one and examined it closely. "These are quite good."

"Carlos Mendez makes them. It's a hard stone to work with."

"I can see that." Matthew placed the item back on the shelf. "Do you miss Savannah?"

"At first I suppose I did, but now I wouldn't know what to do with myself there."

"Have you ever spent any time in New York?"

"No."

"Fascinating place, but far too busy for myself." He moved over to the far wall where some of her lace work and linens were. "Ben said you made some linens for his mother."

"Mo bought them as a wedding gift."

"Right, he mentioned that. Fine boy."

"Yes, he is." What was this man fishing for?

"Miss Martin, let me be honest with you. I'm a widower. My wife passed away two years ago. I have a son named Micah. We were never blessed with any other children. I'm a decent man, make a fair wage for my labors, and I was wondering if you'd do me the honor of your company for dinner this evening."

"What?" Peg nearly fell off her stool.

"I find you an attractive woman, but that isn't what interests me. The fact that you passed out at the very sight of me—well, that can make a man be fascinated with a woman. Granted, I'm certain it wasn't my stunning looks that made you swoon."

"You look fine." Had she really let that slip out? Judging from the smile upon his face, she had. Her face reheated for the second time in a few short minutes.

"Ah, so it's not the hideous growth on my back that caused you to pass out," he chuckled.

Peg couldn't help but laugh. The man had to be the most handsome man she'd seen in a long time. Plenty of men passed through Key West, but none distinguished themselves quite like Matthew. "I don't keep company with men."

"You. . .your brother did tell me that. I forgot. Forgive me, Ma'am. I was so taken in by your beauty, I simply forgot myself." He bowed and grinned.

"What are you after, Mr. Bower?"

"A chance to become friends. If anything else develops we'll leave it in the Lord's hands, but I'm simply reaching out as a friend. Most folks are paired up here."

That was true enough. The seamen that came to port weren't the kind to settle down, but most other folks married young. Peg fanned herself. How did he do it? She was so flustered just being in the man's presence.

"I've been here for ten minutes, and you haven't passed out or run in the other direction. I'm making progress, I see." Matthew flashed his handsome, twisted grin, and Peg felt gooseflesh rise on her body all the way down to her toes. No one had ever affected her like that. Well, no one since Billy, she amended.

Peg chuckled. "You're positively incorrigible."

"Another one of my endearing qualities. Although Esther did find it annoying a time or two."

"Was Esther your wife?" She was interested; she couldn't help herself.

"Yes, we were married for twenty years. A good marriage.

We had our ups and downs, but God was good, and we worked through most things."

"What happened? If you don't mind me asking." Peg placed the blanket on the counter.

Matthew edged closer and reached out to touch the embroidered heron. "You do marvelous work, Miss Martin. I've never seen anything finer. May I see the other side?"

"No, it isn't as pretty because there is a lining to cover it."

"Ah, much like ourselves, hey?"

Peg shielded her eyes. How could he know this about her? She was a fairly decent looking woman, although age was taking its toll. But on the inside she was still a mess. A scarred mess from the bad choices she'd made years ago. No one knew. Only her parents, and they were gone, and her brother Daniel. No one else.

"Sorry, didn't mean to be so personal. It's just how I see myself. I have a great facade, but some of my inner thoughts, my secrets, need to remain hidden from anyone else's eyes."

"Did you know my family in Savannah?" Peg pushed.

"No, I'm afraid I didn't. It's a fairly good-sized city and, unless your father was in the same line of work as myself, I can't imagine our paths crossing."

"Dad was a fisherman."

"That explains your love for the water."

"How did you know?" she asked a little too quickly, amazed that for the second time she'd spoken her thoughts rather than kept them to herself.

"The view. You're the only residential business on the harbor. Everything else is commercial."

"I got the place during the war. A wrecker was calling it quits."

"A wrecker?"

"Oh, that's the name they gave the folks who salvaged the goods from sinking ships. The reefs around the island fool quite a few sailors. It was a great business until the war. Then the soldiers stopped it. Of course, the increase of naval vessels in the area stopped a lot of the groundings, and the light stations helped as well."

"So wreckers were pirates?"

"Goodness, no. It was very legal. They recovered material from the boats and were paid by the company that owned it, or their insurance company, or by the folks who bought it. Either way, a judge had to decide who got which wrecking permit. Mostly it was done in order, but from time to time a man would come in with a sighting and simply stake the claim. In other words, it was salvaging."

"Ah. I think I understand now. So, what do you say about having dinner with me?"

"Like I said before, I don't—"

"Keep company with men. I know. I just thought once you got to know me a bit you might change your mind. Besides, I'm not really looking for a romantic dinner for two, just someone to have some conversation with. Do you go out to dinner with friends?"

"Sometimes."

"Well, don't I deserve your friendship after I saved your life?"

"My life?" Peg wagged her head in disbelief.

"Ah, but, Ma'am, I caught your head in my hands mere seconds before it came crashing down on this hard floor." He winked.

"You *are* incorrigible." Peg smiled in spite of herself.

"I try. Please say you'll do me the honor of eating dinner with me. It's so boring to eat alone."

"I'm really sorry, but I've already made plans for the evening."

"Fair enough. But be advised, I shall return, and I will ask again." He nodded slightly, then winked before turning around and exiting the store.

"Thank You, Lord, for dinner plans." She didn't know how she could have turned down Matthew's request. He had a way about him that just. . .just what? Made her feel so on edge she felt like she was going to explode? That her past could come crashing down around her heels at any time? Or was it more simple than that? Was he awakening in her desires she thought long ago buried? She closed her eyes and breathed in deeply. That was probably the case. He represented a threat to all the decisions she'd made in her life. Decisions that had kept her well for many years. Decisions that kept her alone and never quite forgiven.

Oh sure, she knew God's grace covered the multitude of her past sins and present ones. But she couldn't forgive herself. Not now, not ever. She'd made foolish choices. Costly choices, and they had long-term consequences.

"Enough," she fumed. "I buried the past with You, Lord. Please take this guilt away. I can't deal with it any longer." Her son was dead, and it was all her fault.

Peg locked the door to the shop and slipped into the narrow back room where she knelt down in front of an old wooden chair and cried. Cried for her past. Cried for her son. Cried for the life she'd lost. "Oh, God, it still hurts after all these years. Why? How much longer do I have to wait for healing?"

❧

Came on a little strong there, didn't you, Bower? Perhaps he should have tried a less forward approach. But it did demonstrate one thing. She might not be the same Margaret Martin he was looking for. *Who are you kidding, Bower? She's the one. There's no question, and you know it.*

Matthew walked up to a palm tree and leaned against it. He was due at the Southards' dinner party in half an hour. He'd hoped to bring Peg with him, but she'd refused just like Daniel said she would.

Did her past dictate her current choices? Obviously. *Twenty years, Lord. Hasn't the woman learned to cope with it by now?* He sighed. *Lord, I've only known for a couple months, and I'm barely coping with it. What will she do once she learns the truth? Maybe I shouldn't tell her.*

Matt headed toward the shoreline. Mounds of black eel-grass lined the shore. White puffs of churned up sea-foam draped the edges of the grass. Black and white, side by side, each contrasting the other, each having a part in the beauty of the ocean. They told a symbolic story that made him smile. Black stripes of sin cover us, but the white cleansing foam of Jesus washes the many sins of our lives and pulls them out to sea to be buried in the sea of God's forgetfulness.

Okay, Lord, I get Your point. I'll wait, but give me the words when the time comes. I can't imagine how this truth will rip apart this woman's heart. It's ripping mine. Matthew bent down and pulled up a handful of the eelgrass and tossed it in the ocean. *Help me get close to her, Lord. She needs a friend. Of course, when I tell her what I know, she'll not want to talk with me again.*

He rinsed his hands in the water and walked down the shore. Ellis Southard's house was down this way and up a few blocks. The long walk would do him some good, Matt reasoned.

"Hey, Mr. Bower."

Matt turned to see Ben waving. He appeared to be walking

with his entire family. Mo Greene stood head and shoulders above any man he'd ever known, but the few times Matt had met him he seemed to have a gentle spirit. "Hi, Ben, Mo."

"Ya comin' to Mr. Ellis's for dinner?"

"Sure am. Are you?" Matt headed toward the family.

Mo extended his hand. "You're welcome to walk with us. Matt Bower, this be my beautiful wife, Lizzy."

"Pleasure to meet you, Ma'am."

"Nice to meet you too, Mr. Bower. Ben's told us so much about you."

Matt grinned. He'd hired the boy a few times over the past couple of weeks since arriving to the island.

"And these are our young'uns. Ben you know. This here is Sarah, William, and Olivia."

"Pleasure meeting all of you."

"Do you really sell cotton that slaves picked for you?" Sarah knitted her eyebrows and crossed her arms over her chest.

"Since slavery is against the law, I don't suppose I do. But I did when it wasn't against the law."

"Sarah," Lizzy chastised.

"It's all right, Ma'am. It's an honest question. Don't know many men who didn't make a living using slaves in the South. I won't go talking politics, but I honestly never saw it as folks from the North did prior to the war. War makes a man think, some good thoughts, some bad. In the end, I surmised the Bible says a man shouldn't own another man. So I realize we were wrong. I'm afraid it doesn't change the way things were, but I feel I've wrestled with it and come to an understanding of my sin in this area. Can you share the table with a man who owned slaves?" Matt asked.

He watched Mo put a hand around his wife's shoulders.

"Ye bein' honest, I suppose we can accept your word for how you were and how you feel now."

"Thank you. Did it take you long to feel a whole man, Mo?"

"Took some time. How'd you know?"

"The scars on your wrist are a dead give away, but I've read some of the abolitionists' works."

Lizzy relaxed her shoulders. "Who have you read?"

"Frederick Douglass, mostly."

The small parade made their way toward Ellis Southard's home. "Lizzy has me reading some of his work now," Mo said. "He explains it well."

"I was afraid you'd say that." Matt's lips twisted ruefully.

Mo slapped him on the back. "I think I like you, Mr. Bower, even if you owned slaves."

"Did you beat your slaves like Daddy's master?" Olivia looked horrified.

"No. I never beat another man nor did I order any beatings. But I did have men who worked for me that did. Once I found out, I fired them and hired others." Matt's stomach tightened. It was hard facing his past. He'd owned slaves. At the time, he didn't even have an inclination that it was wrong. It was so socially acceptable. Slowly, he was beginning to learn that what might be acceptable to men wasn't necessarily acceptable to God. These Negroes had every right to hate him. He represented all the heartaches their people had gone through, and yet they were willing to share a table with him.

"You didn't tell me you owned slaves." Ben sidled up beside him and whispered.

"I'm sorry. You didn't ask. Does that mean you don't want to work for me anymore?"

"Hard to say. My father died fighting people like you."

Matt nodded. "I lost a brother, a father, and a dozen cousins to that war too, some on both sides."

"Some slave owners fought for the Union army?"

"Yes, families were torn apart. Some may never recover because of their pride."

"Which side did your brother fight for?"

"The South."

"Oh." Ben slumped his shoulders.

"Like I said before, Ben. I can't change the past. I can only choose to learn from it and move forward."

Ben paused in the road and scrutinized him. He bit his lower lip, then spoke. "You've been fair to me. I guess I can still work for ya—iffin Mo and Momma don't mind."

Matt sighed. Judging from how uncomfortable he was at this very moment, how much more discomfort would Peg Martin feel when he told her why he'd come to Key West?

four

Peg washed the tears from her face and changed her dress. Tonight she would be having dinner with the Southards, and she didn't need to look like something just washed up on shore. She slipped the baby blanket into a cloth sack she had made for Bea for carrying diapers and a change of clothes for the baby. The same blue heron she'd put on the blanket also stood proudly on the sack. It could also make a handy bag once the child was old enough to carry things to the shore or whatever, she mused.

Peg nibbled her lower lip. Perhaps it was making these items for little James had bought back those memories—not the fact that a handsome stranger from Savannah, Georgia, had been paying her some attention. How could he know her shame? It wasn't at all logical.

Peg slipped the blanket into the sack and pulled the drawstring closed. She took in a deep breath, straightened her skirt, and marched toward the Southards'. Tonight was for rejoicing, rejoicing in God's grace and His gift to the Southard family.

Peg smiled at the sound of the muted voices drifting from the house. Ellis had a penchant for doing things on a large scale. A small dinner party would turn up half the town, if Bea didn't put her foot down. Peg chuckled under her breath. Who could have stopped him? He was so proud, holding this first party to announce their new son. He'd been beaming since the day he discovered Bea was with child.

"Evening, Miss Peg." Richie bounced out from behind the

railing of the porch.

"Evening, Richie."

"Is that for James?" he asked. His blue-gray eyes sparkled with excitement.

"It is."

"Nanna is going to love that. Did you make it?"

"Yes."

Richie nodded his head up and down and placed his hands behind his back, then looked down at his feet.

"Has James received a lot of presents?"

"Nanna says, for a little while folks will be giving James lots of presents. Then, after awhile, it will only be on his birthday, like me."

"I see. So, this little item I have in my purse—you would like me to wait to give it to you on your birthday?"

Richie's grin beamed. "You brought me a present? Yippee! Can I open it?"

"You'd better ask Nanna or Uncle Ellis."

Richie ran off hollering, "Nanna, Uncle Ellis."

Peg reached the front door, chuckling to herself, and knocked. Bea had told her often how she couldn't keep the boy still. Thankfully, most of the time he didn't run in the house.

"Peg, I'm so glad you came." Bea hugged her friend. The deep shadows under her eyes revealed volumes. "Come in, come in and join the crowd."

"Ellis got carried away again, I see."

"I don't think Cook or I could have held him down on this one. But he promised me that I was free to escape into our room if the evening wore on too long."

"Good, you look as though you could use some rest."

"James was up half the night. He's a good baby but. . ." her words trailed off.

Peg picked them up. "But you won't mind when he's sleeping through the night."

"Exactly."

"I've missed you. I haven't been to town for ages." Bea draped a hand around Peg's waist.

"The shop's been busy. I meant to come before now. I just haven't had the time." Peg walked in step with her friend. "Oh, I made a little something for you—and James, of course."

Peg handed her the gift. "It's beautiful. And the heron is the same color as Ellis and Richie's eyes. How'd you do that?"

"A special blend of thread."

"You're so creative, Peg. This is wonderful."

Bea took the gift and showed it to Cook, who fingered the fine work with knowing hands. Her deep brown skin accented the white linen. "Mighty fine work, Miz Peg," Cook offered. "My eyes are getting too dim to do fancy work like this."

Peg was flattered, but she knew Cook could still weave a needle as fast as the best of them. Peg had sat in on several quilting sessions where folks were making quilts and linens for the displaced slaves. Lizzy, Cook's daughter, had begun the project shortly after she married Mo Greene.

The sack passed from woman to woman, and praises mingled with statements on how they were going to do more shopping at Southern Treasures and save themselves some time. She wouldn't mind the additional business, but Peg knew they were just being nice. Most folks didn't have the kind of money to buy too many of her gifts. She tried to keep costs down, but they were labor-intense projects.

Peg whispered into Bea's ear. "When you get the sack back, you might want to look inside."

Bea smiled. "I did. It's wonderful."

"Now, where's this handsome son Ellis has been bragging

about?" Peg scanned the room.

"Upstairs taking a nap. Come on. I need to check on him anyway."

The two women headed up the stairs. "Oh, I brought a little something for Richie," Peg offered as they stepped into the hallway on the second floor.

"Is that what he was hollering about?"

"Afraid so. I hope he's not disappointed. It's just some penny candy and a top."

"He'll love it."

Bea opened the bedroom door. Inside, the white bassinet was covered with fine white mosquito netting. Bugs were a problem on the island but manageable. Bea lifted a finger to her lips. "Shh," she whispered.

Peg nodded and stepped lightly on her toes, avoiding the click her heels would make on the hardwood flooring.

James's toothless grin looked up at them.

"Guess he wasn't asleep." Bea fussed with the netting and retrieved her son.

Peg's heart tightened. "He's beautiful."

"I'm kind of partial," Bea smiled. "Would you like to hold him?"

"May I?"

"Of course. He'll be asking for his supper shortly. Let me run downstairs and tell Ellis I'll be feeding James."

Peg sat down on the rocker and cradled her arms to receive the tiny infant. Bea scurried out of the room. Tears nipped at Peg's eyes as she fought to hold them back. "My, my, James, aren't you a handsome lad."

The baby cooed.

Peg removed the hoods from the baby's hands and caressed the tiny fingers. He wrapped his fingers around her much larger one and held on tight.

He turned his head toward her breast. Peg lifted him higher. "Your mommy will be here shortly." She caressed his soft cheek and kissed him tenderly on his forehead.

"You look so much like I pictured my own son." A tear slipped past her eyelids and ran down her cheek.

"Peg?" Bea whispered and closed the door. "You have a son?"

☙

Matt couldn't believe the crowd in Ellis Southard's home. It appeared to be just about everyone who lived on the island. They all mingled—white, black, Hispanic—everyone together in one room. Since the war began, he'd been trying to understand how folks could look at others without considering race and equality. Yet here on a tiny remote island in the middle of nowhere, the people had figured it out. Matt held his glass and saluted the heavens. *I finally got it, Lord. Thanks.*

Mo Greene walked up to him. The pure size of the former slave could make a man quake in his boots. Matt squared his footing. "Quite a crowd."

"Mr. Ellis doesn't hold back when he celebrates," Mo agreed.

"I can see that."

"I wanted to apologize for Sarah's behavior earlier."

"Nothing to apologize for, Mo. She spoke from her heart."

"The young'uns have been born free. They don't know what it's like to speak only when spoken to, to not look a white man in the eye."

Matt noticed Mo had no trouble looking him in the eye. "You escaped, didn't you?"

"Yes, Sir."

Matt nodded his head. "Those wrists tell a story, Mo. I'm

sorry you were locked in chains."

"The chains weren't nothin' compared to the beatin's."

"I'm sorry, Mo." What else could he say? It wasn't his fault, and yet, by not resisting the inhumanity of slavery, by owning his own slaves even though he'd paid them well, much to the annoyance of his business associates, he had been just as guilty as the men who used the whip.

"You understand, don't you?" Mo placed a hand on Matt's shoulder. Their eyes connected. Volumes of words were shouted between them, though not one was spoken. Mo tapped his hand on Matt's shoulder. "I'm pleased to know you, Mr. Bower."

Matt's voice caught. "Pleasure is all mine." Matt internally winced at the choice of social formalities he'd used. For it certainly wasn't pleasure that stirred in his gut. Acknowledging one's sins was never a pleasurable experience. However, God's grace covered those sins and brought about a cleansing so deep it washed him from head to toe. Matt couldn't wait to have some quiet time with the Lord.

Mo chuckled. "It's hard gettin' used to livin' a new kind of life, but I think you're gettin' there."

Matt wondered, *Am I that transparent, Lord?*

"I'll leave ye to your thoughts." Mo left him standing there in the corner of the room, looking out the picture window to the back gardens of Ellis Southard's property. People were even out there mingling. Just how many folks had Ellis Southard invited?

"Matt. Glad you could make it." Ellis Southard walked into the dining room.

"Thank you for the invitation." Matt raised his glass of limeade.

"You're welcome. I wanted to hear more about the plans

for your business." Ellis grabbed a sandwich from the table and walked up beside him.

"Not much to it. I've decided to relocate. Savannah was devastated by the war, although it is rebuilding. I thought if I could cut down on my expenses and speed up the delivery time by having the cotton arrive here rather than in Savannah, I might be able to still turn a profit."

"So you'd be needing a warehouse, some place close to the harbor."

"That I would. I'm afraid the property is pretty locked up. Most folks who own waterfront property have been making a profit and have no intentions of selling."

"True. But the wrecking business isn't what it used to be before the war, so there may be some property up for a decent price."

"Perhaps." Matt raised his glass to his lips. Maybe exporting was still out of the question. It had been his business before the war, and he'd done well. But with the boycott of Southern goods to the North, and the pirating of ships bound for Europe, he'd barely made anything during the war. Not to mention the fact that Confederate money wasn't worth the paper it had been printed on. "My understanding is that Key West remained under Union control throughout the war."

"Your understanding is correct. The men and women who sided with the South were allowed to leave. Some did. But not too long after that order had been given, it was rescinded. Folks somehow lived harmoniously during the war. That isn't to say a few arguments didn't get passed between the best of friends, but there was no blood shed, and for that I'm grateful."

Ellis Southard was an interesting man. Word on the street was he paid Mo more than most folks earned. And yet his business continued to grow. How could he afford such benevolence?

"So, where's this strapping young man you said was your son?" Matt recalled his own pride and joy at bringing Micah home for the first time.

"His mother is feeding him. Bea said she'd bring him down shortly after he's through." Ellis beamed.

"Children are a blessing from the Lord."

"Amen. You said you have a son?"

"Micah, yes. He makes this father proud."

"I know what you mean. Richie, my nephew, is such a fine young boy. Bea did an excellent job raising him," he added. "My brother and his wife both died, leaving Richie to my care. I know he's not my son, in terms of biology, but I still feel the same pride for him as I do for James. And at the same time, I have the same awareness of what an awesome responsibility God has given me to raise these boys."

"I hear you. I felt similar about raising Micah. He's twenty now, and continuing his education, but he plans on coming here to spend his Christmas holiday with me."

"I look forward to meeting him."

"Ellis," a female voice called.

"Excuse me."

Ellis left, leaving Matt back to his own thoughts. He too felt that same awesome responsibility to raise Micah. Now, he realized, due to someone else's sin, he might lose what he thought was as much a part of him as life itself. Matt fisted his left hand, then flexed his fingers. *God, I don't think I can carry this yoke.*

five

"Peg, what happened to your baby?" Bea asked.

Peg's tears burned a path down her cheek. "Bea, I—I. . ."

Bea sat down beside her and placed an arm lovingly around her shoulders. "I'm sorry, I didn't mean to pry. I just never knew."

"No one does. Well, except my family." Peg sniffled and handed the tiny infant back to his mother. For twenty years she'd kept this secret, and now it was out. Peg closed her eyes and took in a deep breath, then slowly eased it out. Peg's heart tightened again as she watched little James suckle at his mother's breast.

"My child died at birth. I—I never knew him."

"Oh, Peg, how horrible for you. What about your husband?"

Peg twisted the handkerchief in her hands and turned away. How could she admit to her friend what kind of woman she had been?

Bea placed her hand on Peg's. "I understand."

"I'm glad you do; I certainly don't. I wasn't raised that way. I still can't believe I let Billy. . . Well, it was my fault just as much as it was his." Peg got up and started to pace. "We were engaged. Not that it matters any. The minute he found out I was with child he snuck out of town.

"My family had me stay with some relatives once I began to show, but no one could have guessed I would have lost the baby. Dan and I moved to Key West right afterwards. I thought I'd buried my past. But this new stranger to the island,

40

Matthew Bower, something about him—I don't know, I can't put my finger on it—but his being here is bringing it all back. Like my entire shame will be brought to the surface. For twenty years no one has known.

"Just look at me rattling off my tongue with you now about it. I've never said a word to anyone. I barely even talked with Daniel. God took my son because of my sin."

"You can't believe that!"

Peg sat back down beside Bea. "Honestly, I don't know what to believe any more. I had dinner with gentlemen a few times after we arrived, but I figured it was best to keep men at a distance. I don't trust myself."

"Peg, you're not the same naive girl from the past. I don't think it would happen again."

"I don't know. I don't even want to find out. It's best to remain single. Doesn't Paul say something in the Bible about it being a noble calling?"

"Sort of. But still, God is a God of grace. He died for our sins. He doesn't continue to condemn us over and over again."

"I figure God's allowed me to have a peaceful life, a good business. That's His grace for me."

"I'm not going to argue as to whether or not it is God's will for you to remain single or not. I simply couldn't answer that. But Peg, you can't believe God took your son because you sinned. You're not the first to have a child out of wedlock, and you won't be the last, I'm sorry to say."

"Maybe you're right. I guess it really has nothing to do with Matthew Bower being from Savannah. Maybe it has to do with the fact that it's the twentieth anniversary of my son's birth and death. He cried so loudly when he was born. It was so hard to believe he lost his life mere moments later.

I don't know what I would have done if not for the love of my family."

"God would have gotten you through it. What day was he born?"

"November twenty-eighth at six o'clock in the morning. It was a long night. I started labor early the afternoon before." Peg went on to explain the long labor, the need to be at the doctor's home, and the doctor's face when he told her the news. "He just confirmed what everyone's opinion was about a single girl having a child. Granted, it was a mistake, and I shouldn't have allowed myself to get into such a predicament in the first place, but—"

"But one sinner was condemning another."

"Right. I know I was wrong, but to have people condemning me on top of my own condemnation. . . It was a horrible time. That's why Daniel suggested we move here. A new place, a fresh start. No one would know. No one would care."

"So what does Matt Bower have to do with all of this?"

"Nothing, other than the fact that he hails from Savannah. I've avoided contact with folks from Savannah. Didn't want word to get out."

"Peg, my lips are sealed. I won't tell a soul. It's a matter between you and the Lord. But I'm here if you ever want to talk about it. Especially with the birth date coming up in a couple weeks."

"Those are my hardest days. Every year I relive what might have been. I know God has forgiven me, but I can't forgive myself."

"You must. You need to be free of the past." Bea squeezed her hand. "Twenty years is a long time."

"I know. I can't believe I told you everything."

Bea smiled. "Guess it's because you trusted me."

"Nah, it's because you caught me with my guard down."

Bea chuckled. "Probably."

Peg sniffed and dabbed her nose with her handkerchief.

James finished his dinner, and Bea handed him over to Peg to burp him. The tiny infant seemed so strong in her arms. She placed the cloth over her shoulder and lightly began to tap the baby's back.

"What would you do if the Lord placed a man into your life, Peg?" Bea asked, making herself presentable.

"Thankfully, I don't have to wonder about that. I know He won't. I've accepted the fact that I'm to remain single."

"Hmm, I wonder." Bea's eyes sparkled with mischievous intent.

&

Matt placed his empty glass on a tray and headed for the door. He'd spent enough time at Ellis Southard's to be able to leave yet still be socially appropriate.

"Mr. Bower," Nathaniel Farris called out to him.

Not quite fast enough, he inwardly sighed, and put the social smile back up on his face. "Mr. Farris, how nice to see you."

"Pleasure's all mine. I heard you were looking to buy some waterfront property."

Word certainly does travel quickly on this small island, he thought. "Yes, do you know of some?"

"Not really. Jefferson Scott has a piece that he might be willing to rent. Don't believe he has a mind to sell. At least not yet."

"I see. And where might Mr. Scott's property be?"

"Do you know where Southern Treasures is located?"

Matt nodded his head.

"The dock behind the store front. Actually, he owns the

building the store is in also."

Of all the property on this little berg, it had to be Peg Martin's. "I thought Peg Martin owned it."

"The store, yes, but the building, no. Of course, she's a great tenant, and that added income would be helpful for launching a new business."

"True." But Matt needed more than just a pier, he needed a building for storage of the goods between shipments. And he'd been inside that storefront more than once; it was too small for what he needed. Of course, he could build a second, and possibly a third floor. Matt scratched his five o'clock shadow. "Where might I find this Jefferson Scott? And speaking of buildings, who owns yours?" Matt added.

Nathaniel paled. "You wouldn't be—"

Matt chuckled. "No, it's too small, and too far from the harbor. I heard folks saying you might be asking Peg Martin for her hand in marriage."

"What?" Nathaniel swayed his head from side to side. "This island's grapevine can kill a man."

"Interesting term to use regarding marriage." Matt toyed with him. All the same, it was interesting he would mention Peg Martin's property if he were going to ask for her hand in marriage. Perhaps he hoped to keep his wife at home. Not that Matt could blame him; Esther had stayed at home raising Micah. But she had worked in her own way, arranging their social calendar, hosting dinner parties and endless other social occasions that helped a man's business grow and succeed.

"Peg Martin is a dear friend, but there is no truth to the rumor." Nathaniel looked uncomfortable.

"Ah, I see." And he did. Rumors and rumor mills abounded in small towns, and in large ones, for that matter. If he didn't know that to be true, then why had he kept his intent for coming to Key West such a secret? Because he knew how gossip spread. And no matter what the doctor had done of his own free will, Matt knew he'd have to live in the shadows of that doctor's decision for the rest of his life. Folks were bound to talk once the truth was told. And Micah might never have a future here as a result. Perhaps Matt should reconsider. After all, no one knew except himself.

࿊

Peg washed her face and dabbed it dry with a hand towel. Bea had left her alone in the nursery to collect her thoughts. In some small way, she felt better to have someone know her secret. *Would she tell?* Peg nibbled her lower lip. *No, not Bea. Someone else, possibly, but never Bea.*

Straightening her hair in the mirror, she practiced a smile. It looked fake, but she had no choice. Half the town was here, or so it seemed. Maybe she could sneak out while Bea and Ellis were showing off James. She clutched her drawstring purse and forced herself to leave the quiet walls of the nursery.

Laughter filled the air. Peg clutched the railing. No, she chided herself, they weren't laughing at her. She stepped down another stair.

Ellis's voice boomed above the rest, and the house went silent. Folks looked toward the dinning room where Bea stood beside her husband. The happy couple. Had it only been a couple years since Bea arrived to Key West?

Peg's eyes drifted over the crowd. Folks were paired off. Mo and Lizzy stood proudly in a corner. Lizzy's swollen belly spoke of the love and new life she and Mo had. Toward the back wall and close to the front door stood Matthew Bower. He looked as out of place as she felt.

His eyes glanced up the stairway and locked with her own.

Peg's palms began to sweat. She rolled her shoulders back and took another step down.

Matt gave her a solitary nod and broke their gaze. He focused on Ellis.

Peg tried to hear the words, but they were muffled by her own inner thoughts and turmoil. She fought off her fear and took another step down, one step closer to the front door. Did she really want to walk past Matthew Bower? Her hand tightened again on the railing.

The crowd erupted into laughter and cheers. James started to cry, and Bea jiggled her son on her shoulder. The room calmed and folks resumed their conversations with each other in hushed and whispered tones.

Cook stood proudly at the bottom of the stairs as Peg stepped down the remaining steps. "Cook, please tell Miz Bea I've an order I just have to finish, and thank her for the kind invitation."

"Certainly. Are ya feelin' all right, Child?"

"Fine. Just exhausted getting ready for Christmas orders."

"I imagine so. I'll give Miz Bea the message."

"Thank you, Cook." Peg sidestepped to the front door.

"Allow me." Matt Bower opened the door for her and bowed slightly. *A gentleman—what's a man like that doing in Key West?* she wondered to herself.

"May I escort you home or to your business?" Matt asked.

No, she wanted to scream. Didn't he know he was the source of her discomfort? Of course not, he didn't have a speck of knowledge. And yet there was something in his vivid green eyes. "Home," she answered.

He held out his elbow for her to slip her hand within its crook. His arm seemed strong and firm below the layers of his clothing. She clasped tighter.

Matt placed his hand upon hers and patted it. "Your honor is safe with me, Miss Martin."

Honor? He had no idea how little she actually had. Peg bit her inner cheek and nodded her agreement to his escort. They stepped down the stairs and walked out the small driveway to Front Street.

"Nathaniel Farris mentioned that Jefferson Scott might be interested in selling his waterfront property."

Peg stopped, pulling Matt Bower to a halt. "You're going to buy my building?"

six

"I need a pier, but the building is too small for my purposes," Matt told her.

Peg stayed firmly planted. Matt tried to move her forward, but she resisted his gentle encouragement.

"Why are you doing this to me?"

Her golden hair glittered in the lamplight. "I'm not doing anything to you, as you say. I'm simply looking for a place where I can conduct my business. Your building quite possibly may be the answer to my prayers."

"But. . ."

"Look, you have a quaint business. But I need a place to store and distribute my goods from. Personally, the property is too small for my needs, but perhaps I could build upon it."

"You'd tear it down?"

"Progress, Miss Martin, progress. You must think in those terms."

"Progress? You can't be serious. I've been in that location for seven years. I'm bringing in a fair salary for my work."

"I don't doubt that. You've some fine merchandise. But my business would employ folks from the town. Yours simply gives them some extra pocket change every once in awhile. Besides, you don't need to be located on the waterfront, whereas it is essential for my business to be located there. You could move yours further up Duval Street, no harm done. Mine couldn't be anywhere else."

"Is this why you came into my store earlier today? Did

you ask me to go out with you simply to tell me of your grand plans to ruin my business?"

"What was in the limeade you were drinking? I'm simply letting you know I will be speaking with Jefferson Scott on the morrow. I certainly didn't want you to assume I would go behind your back regarding the property."

She bent her head down. "I'm sorry," she mumbled.

Matt calmed his inner thoughts. Knowing the truth didn't set a man free; it bound him tighter than a bale of cotton. "Apology accepted. And I apologize for any offense I might have caused you. I must say, we have quite a way with each other. The first moment you see me you faint, and now—"

"Correction, it wasn't the first time. I noticed you after you departed the ship."

Matt grinned. "Ah, it must have been my captivating good looks. It causes all the women's heads to turn."

She shot him a sideways glance, and he chuckled. She giggled and recaptured his arm. "It must have been."

"But, Madam, you must not swoon at my feet. For, alas, my heart belongs to another."

Peg released his arm.

"I'm a widower, Peg," he explained. "I still love my wife. We had many cherished years together."

Peg recaptured his offered elbow. "Yes, you mentioned that earlier."

"So you see, your honor is safe with me." Matt flashed his million-dollar grin. Getting to know this woman would take all the understanding he could muster. Esther had easy been to read. Or so he'd thought. She did manage to keep her illness hidden from him for a year. Looking back now, he saw how she hid the truth from him.

"I have no doubt you are a gentleman, Mr. Bower."

"Tell me about your island." Matt hoped if her tongue loosened about something simple, that might help build a bridge to one day allow them to. . . To what? What did he hope to accomplish by telling this woman anything? He fought the tension rising in his spine.

"There's not too much to tell. The island was first a part of Cuba and thus a part of Spain. It was a gift to Juan Pablo Salas as a thanksgiving for his services. He immediately sold the place to Mr. Simoneton from Connecticut. Prior to that it was a watering hole for ships passing through the region. I've been told it's on some of the oldest maps of the area. Today, cisterns are a major part of most households, but back then there was fresh water on the island. The government is involved with removing the salt out of the water for fresh drinking water. But it's a costly task. Thankfully, there is a good rainy season, and the cisterns hold us well."

"How many folks would you say now live on the island?"

"Around four thousand. Back in the thirties John Audubon was here, painting and drawing the birds and animals of the island."

"Were you here then? You must have been a child."

Peg's lips curled upward into a delicate smile. "No, my brother and I arrived about twenty years ago."

"Esther and I arrived in Savannah about that time. I was bringing my wife home from the North where I attended business school. My father, a true Southern gentleman, couldn't believe I'd educate myself in the North. But he loved Esther and decided, if for nothing else, my education in the North brought him a fine daughter-in-law."

"If I'm not imposing, what happened to Esther?" she asked with tender compassion.

"She had an illness that caused her great pain. The doctor

said he'd seen it before, but there was nothing to cure her. It was as if her insides were dying before they should. Unfortunately, the pain became so great that her medicine took control of her body. Her last months were exhausting, and with the war in full swing, little could be done. Her suffering tested my faith in a merciful God in ways I never dreamed possible."

Peg tightened her grip of his arm. "I'm sorry. Losing someone close to you is a terrible pain."

Matt tapped the top of her hand. "But the good Lord gets us through it."

"Yes, yes, He does," she whispered.

Matt stopped at the end of Front Street. "Where do we go from here?"

"Oh, sorry. I wasn't paying attention. I live up Duval a couple of blocks. My brother and I purchased the home shortly after we arrived on the island. I have a small apartment, and he and his new wife live in the main part of the house. Carmen was a widow with three young children when Daniel met her."

"A brave man to take on an entire family."

"Seems to be a lot of that going around after the war. So many families left without husbands and fathers."

"True. War rips at the very heart of a family. I lost my father and brother during the war. Thankfully, my son was spared. By the time he was old enough to fight, the war was ending. At least it had ended in Savannah."

"I understand the North took Fort Pulaski in 1862? How did that affect the city?"

"Just about ruined us. My business, by virtue of its trade, was perhaps one of the hardest hit. Shipping cotton became a primary target of the North. They didn't want us earning money to reinforce the troops with supplies."

Peg nodded soberly. "We were spared bloodshed on the

island. As soon as word got out that Florida was seceding from the Union, Captain J. M. Brannan marched on Fort Zachary Taylor and took possession of it for the North. He actually sent for reinforcements before he marched. So it wasn't long before additional troops from the North came here."

Peg halted. "This is my home. Thank you for the escort. It wasn't necessary, but it was nice to get to know you a bit."

"Pleasure was all mine. I'd love to visit with you again, if you don't find that being too forward." Peg Martin was easy to talk with. Perhaps he could establish a relationship with her of some sort that would help him build up to telling her why he'd really come to this remote island. Of course, there might be no need to tell her at all. It might simply not matter.

Who are you fooling? he chided himself. He, more than anyone, knew the importance of the information he had. She would want to know. She had a right to know. *Didn't she?*

"Good night, fair lady, may your dreams be blessings from our heavenly Father, gifts of mercy, peace, and joy." Matt kissed the top of her hand and departed.

Why on earth did you do that, Bower? Now the woman will never want to see you again. She'll be certain you're after a romantic relationship. Was he? No, he had been a happily married man. One only finds true love once in his lifetime, and Esther was that love. But the golden image of Margaret Martin fused in his mind as he watched the silver moon edge past the palm trees that lined the road. Was he ready for another relationship? No, he couldn't be. Esther had only been gone for a little over two years. And what about Micah? What would he say?

"Micah, I miss you, Son," he whispered into the night air.

⁂

Peg unlocked the door to her small apartment. A part of her

missed the full use of the house, but it had been practical for Daniel and Carmen to have the majority of the dwelling. She often wondered if Daniel had put off marriage because of her and her past. Just how many lives does one sin affect? Peg closed her eyes and blinked back the tears. No, she wouldn't cry again. After all, she'd opened her heart to Bea—wasn't that enough?

Peg filled a kettle with water and placed it on the stove. Lighting a small fire, she got comfortable for the evening.

Matthew Bower seemed like a fine man. She looked down at her right hand where he had kissed it. She'd been kissed many times in formal greetings, but never had she experienced the warmth that traveled up her arm as his lips touched her skin. Now, Peg fought off a chill that ran through her body.

Oh, admit it—he's handsome and nice, and you're attracted to him. She heard the water boiling in the kettle and poured a cup into an old mug she'd had for years. She dropped in a pinch of English breakfast tea leaves, her favorite, and brought the mug to the living room, where she lit a small oil lamp and fished out some needlework from her bag beside her chair.

Needlework by day and night. "You really should get out and enjoy life, Peg," she said out loud. "And speaking to yourself is a sure sign of senility." Perhaps being social with Matthew Bower wasn't such a bad idea after all.

Peg picked up her tea and sipped it slowly. Had she really not accepted God's grace and forgiveness for her past sins, as Bea had indicated earlier?

She scanned the solitary apartment. Bare walls, no paintings of family members or loved ones. Nothing more than a few hangings she had made to try and brighten up the place in a small way. The muffled laughter from the rooms next door revealed her empty life tonight. Life had moved on without her. She'd kept herself on the sidelines, refusing to accept that life could be different, that God's forgiveness covered a multitude of sins, including hers.

"Lord, I don't understand why Matthew Bower affects me so. Why am I so afraid of him and yet feel so comfortable with him? How can life be so confusing? Neither one of us is looking for a relationship, a romance. You know I could never have another romance with a man. But I would like to establish a friendship with him, if that is all right. He seems like a fair man, an honest man. Oh, but don't let him buy my building. I couldn't possibly afford to rent a store in town."

Peg finished off her prayer time with a few moments of reading God's Word. By the time her tea was finished and her daily readings were done, it was time for bed. For the first time in days she felt peace. Real peace. A God-given peace that allowed her spirit to calm.

❧

A few days later, the sun shone brightly through her sheer white curtains, greeting her with a kiss of sunshine. Life was good. The anniversary of her son's birth weighed less upon her shoulders as the fateful day approached. Opening her heart to Bea had been a wonderful release, a reminder that not all condemn, and that some even show compassion when others stumble.

She was spending less and less time with Daniel and Carmen, having resolved they needed their own private time to build their new family. But each day she'd run into Matt Bower. Their friendship grew slowly, very slowly. He still set her on edge when he was around. It didn't make sense—the man was a perfect gentleman. Yet possibly that was the problem. He seemed almost too perfect, although he did admit to his own shortcomings, like being unaware of his wife's illness for nearly a year.

Micah, she learned, was his son. *There couldn't be a
prouder father,* she thought. He positively beamed when he
spoke of the boy. But he wasn't a boy any longer; he was a
man, twenty years of age. *Could it be that I'm jealous of
Matt and his relationship with his son simply because his son
is nearly the same age as mine would have been?*

Peg dusted the ceramic pottery Gus Witchell had made for
the shop. Matt was right; her trinkets did bring in pennies
compared to what a thriving business could do for several
families on the island. *Should I consider relocating?*

"Penny for your thoughts?" Nathaniel stepped up to her.

"I've got to get that bell back up on the door," Peg teased.

"Why'd you take it down?"

"To polish it. But I never got around to putting it back up.
So, what can I do for you today, Nate?"

He fished an envelope from his pocket. "I received a letter
from Julie."

"What did it say?" Peg made herself comfortable on the
stool behind the counter.

"She apologized for not spending an evening with me and
said she felt unworthy of becoming my wife."

"Did she tell you why?"

"No, not really, just words. . .like she wasn't the same
woman I once knew. It's all very strange."

Peg nibbled her lower lip. Should she tell him what she
suspected? "Nate, have you ever known a woman who was,
was. . ." How could she put this tenderly? "Who'd fallen prey
to a man's unwanted advances?"

Nathaniel's eyebrows came together and creased his forehead. "No, I suppose I never have. Are you saying. . . ?"

"I'm not saying anything except that I am seeing signs of a

woman who may have been attacked."

Nathaniel crumpled the letter in his hand. Red infused his pale features. Peg leaned over and placed her hand upon his. "Nate, if she's feeling unworthy, perhaps something happened to her. Women feel an incredible shame when something like this happens."

He grabbed her hand and held it tightly. "If that be the case, I have some rather unholy thoughts toward the man who, who. . ."

"That's natural too. Pray, and write Julie again. Tell her that no matter what has happened you still love her and want her to be your wife."

"Why would her family not allow me to see her if that were the case?"

"Some families feel ashamed. In some cases, they believe their daughter or sister allowed it to happen. If she were a victim of an unthinkable act, they may not believe she was totally innocent."

"That's ludicrous."

"No, that's shame and guilt. A father feels he should have protected his daughter more. A mother feels she should have been more watchful. And on and on it goes. Some families work through it. Some kick the daughter out and turn her to the streets. I suspect since she's still with her family, they will work it out. But you and I both know your social standing in New York, and her family may assume that your family would not accept tainted goods."

"Hogwash! My family would never even need to know."

"Nathaniel, write her again. Tell her your heart. Give her a chance to heal. I may be all wrong. Possibly nothing has happened. But if something has, I know you're a man with a tender heart and would want to help Julie heal."

"You're a good friend, Peg. How did you acquire such wisdom?"

Because I've been there. "Just watched and listened over the years. You hear all sorts of problems. It's nothing more than any other lady would have told you."

"Perhaps."

"Go write another letter. Give her time to respond and see what she says. If she still loves you, then I suspect she'll come around."

"I should have just brought her with me when I came. Forget the formal ideas of a year's engagement and such. None of this would have happened," he mumbled.

"Now don't you go blaming yourself for what might or might not have happened. You'll be no use to her or yourself."

Peg got up from the stool and came around the counter. She wrapped her arms around Nathaniel and embraced him.

"Thanks, Peg."

"Excuse me," said a voice from the door. "I'm sorry to interrupt."

seven

Peg rolled her eyes at Vivian's grin. It would take hours to convince her that nothing was happening between her and Nathaniel.

"I'd better get back to work. Thanks, Peg. I really appreciate your help," Nate said.

"You're welcome." Peg hustled behind the counter. Why had she felt the need to embrace Nate in the first place? Her foolish actions would have the grapevines humming the rest of the day.

"So, what can I do for you today, Vivian?"

"Nothing really. I just came to browse. I've done my Christmas shopping." Vivian came up to the counter and leaned toward her. "I thought you and Nathaniel were just friends."

"We are. I was just consoling the man."

"Consoling? What is going on?"

"Vivian, you know I can't tell you."

"Oh, phooey. You really are becoming quite a stick in the mud, Peg."

"Just call me 'Stick,' " Peg teased and picked up some needle-point she was working on.

Vivian pulled up another stool. "Seriously, Peg, there's nothing going on between you two?"

"Nothing."

"What about the new man in town, Matt Bower? Folks are saying he's been beating a path to your shop nearly every day." Vivian wiggled her eyebrows.

"Matt is also a friend. He's from Savannah, where Daniel and I came from."

"Oh, so you're old family friends?"

"No, just have the same area in our backgrounds."

Vivian's shoulders slumped. "Hrumph. Isn't there anything exciting going on?"

Peg wondered if some harmless gossip might be in order to occupy the island's time on someone beside herself. "Heard little James Southard is cooing. Ellis seems certain he's saying Dada."

Vivian chuckled. "He's quite proud. You should see little Richie. You'd think he was just as responsible for the baby as his father."

"Oh? Tell me."

Vivian rattled on about Richie and the many errands he was taking to make certain James was being cared for properly, and how Cook and Bea had to do some creative thinking to keep the boy occupied. But Vivian was only momentarily distracted. "So there's nothing to the rumor that you and Nathaniel are getting married?"

"For the last time, Vivian, no."

Vivian waved her hands. "All right, all right. I can take a hint. It's just that he made this beautiful engagement ring. . ."

"Yes, I know. It is beautiful. The woman he gives it to will know she is loved."

"True. I rather like Nathaniel's way of setting a ring. Nothing overdone, just simply stated, showing the jewels in the best lighting."

Peg pulled the thread through the cloth and tied off the end. "He is quite good."

"I shouldn't keep you, but I was curious."

Peg chuckled. "I could tell."

"Two men wooing you at the same time makes for quite the conversation, Dear."

"Vivian!" Peg groaned.

"Just teasing you. Have a wonderful day. Fancy that, here comes Mr. Bower."

Peg rolled her eyes. She definitely had become the subject of many conversations on the island of late.

"Good morning, Miss Martin. How are you today?" Matt said, removing his derby and holding the door open for Vivian to exit the building.

I'd be better if you and Nathaniel didn't visit quite so often. Peg plopped her work on the counter. "So, what brings you this morning?"

Matt closed the door behind him and stepped further into the store. "I've secured some property for my business."

"That's—" Peg's heart leapt in her chest as she caught Matt's somber expression. His green eyes darted back and forth. "You didn't?"

"I'm sorry, Peg. I had to. It was the only waterfront property available."

Peg looked around the full store. To move everything, the shelving, the inventory. . . The mere thought of it sent dread into the marrow of her bones. "How soon do I need to move?" she mumbled.

"January. I couldn't put you out just before Christmas."

"Thanks, I think."

"Peg." Matt stepped up beside her. "I really tried to find something else."

"I know." She stepped back. Her mind raced for an alternative location.

"I promise I'll help you pack and do whatever I can to help

you set up a new store," he offered.

Like come up with the money? she wanted to scream. "I appreciate the offer. I don't even know where I'll begin."

"Micah's arriving just before Christmas. I'm certain he'll give a hand as well."

"Look, Matt, the island is a great place to get folks to help. I appreciate your offer, but seriously, I don't need it. When the time comes, I'll have more help than I can handle." She turned and marched back behind the counter.

Matt nodded and retreated to the front door. He looked at the slate that told folks she'd be closed on the twenty-eighth of November. "What's this?"

"Oh, nothing, just a personal day. Every so often a person needs to take one." She wasn't about to tell him the importance of that date and what it meant to her.

"Good day, Miss Martin."

"Good day, Mr. Bower." Their fragile relationship had reverted back to formal greetings. She had to move. She definitely didn't like the month of November. Nope, nothing good ever happened in November. At least not to her.

&

You handled that well, Bower. Matt stomped toward town. *And to bring up the notice on her door. You know perfectly well what that day represents, and you're keeping that information from her,* Matt scolded himself. If he kept this up there would be no living with himself.

But what kind of life would. . .

Nope, he couldn't think about that. Too much uncertainty remained. If he started to think in those terms he'd never be able to simply leave the past in the past. He'd have to reveal the truth. But was he man enough to face it once it was revealed? With each passing moment, he was becoming less and less sure of himself.

Enough rambling about things not yet an issue. You've got work to do. Ordering lumber, setting up a construction crew. . . Letters needed to be written. The next few days would keep him hopping. If he was to open his business in Key West by February, he didn't have time for idle thoughts or worries from the past.

"Good morning, William." Matt beamed as he walked into the man's office. "I might have some work for you."

William rolled the edges of his mustache and said, "I heard you bought Jefferson Scott's waterfront property."

Matt chuckled and sat down on the oak chair. "You heard correctly." *I'm glad I told Peg immediately. Nothing is a secret for long on this island.*

"So, what can I help you with?" William pulled out a fresh sheet of paper and a pen.

Matt liked a man always ready for business.

The two men spoke for an hour, talking about materials needed, where to order from, how much from Cuba and how much from the North. All in all, William Horton gave solid advice, and Matt felt certain he would prove to be a valuable asset.

"Heard you were courtin' Miss Martin." William beamed, his handlebar mustache riding up his full cheeks.

"Now that rumor isn't true. Peg has simply been a good friend. But after I bought the place out from under her, I'm not so sure she'll be appreciating my friendship."

"Peg's a great gal. She'll get over it. She's always been a loner. Never spent any time with any fella that I'm aware of. Terrible shame for someone as pretty as her to not have an interest in men."

Apparently that hadn't always been the case, Matt mused.

"She does have a fine store," William said out loud. "I know my wife will be sad to see it close."

"I hope she'll be able to relocate further in town."

"Hmm." William rolled his mustache between his thumb and forefinger. "You know, there might just be the perfect place for her on Duval Street. A block east of the church. It's small but can't be smaller than the size of the place she has now."

"Really? Tell me more."

William scribbled a name and address on a piece of paper. "Here. See John Dixon, that's his address. I believe he owns the place." William handed the torn sheet of paper to Matt.

"Thank you. I hate to have her relocate, but it was the only property that would meet my needs."

"Does appear that way. Let me get on these orders. There's a ship heading to Cuba with the evening tide. I'll get your order out on that ship."

"Wonderful. Thank you again, William." Matthew extended his hand.

William grasped it firmly. "Pleasure's all mine. I hope your business will help our community. It appears like it might be able to."

Matt grinned. In Savannah, his business was like so many others. Here in Key West it would be one of a kind. Yes, God was with him, and he could make this work.

❧

Peg grasped the side of the counter. *Of all the days. . .* She broke her train of thought. Wallowing in self-pity wouldn't help matters. She'd seen the inevitable. There wasn't another piece of property on Key West that would suit Matthew Bower's needs apart from the one she rented.

But today of all days! Why today, Lord? Why?

Peg let out a pent-up breath and decided to close the shop

early. She'd need to find a new place to rent, and she had no spare time unless she closed the shop.

The island, with its large wooden structures around the harbor, seemingly would have lots of available space. But the fact of the matter was that many of the spaces had been owned and operated for years by the same businessmen. Hotels seemed to take up a large section of Greene and Front Streets.

Maybe she should just close up shop and do piecework for folks. They certainly knew where she lived, and she wouldn't have to pay rent for a shop that way. After all, the house was bought and paid for, and it wasn't that far up Duval.

Peg grabbed the accounting books. In order to decide, she would need to look the books over. She'd need to figure her profit, then decide what she truly had available for additional rent.

Lots of math, lots of homework. Numbers had never given her a problem, but to be working such detailed work the eve of her son's birth and death. . . Peg closed her eyes and fought back the painful memories.

November twenty-eighth was the one day she allowed herself to grieve. A solemn day. A day to reflect on the past, the present and the future. Apparently not this year, though. *Future, huh? You've kept yourself from any future, Peg old girl, admit it. And now you're standing two years shy of forty, and you're wondering why.*

Peg lifted the ledgers and turned the sign that said to all the world, "Closed."

Her hand trembled. *One day that might be forever.* Her heart tightened in her chest. She fought the bile in her stomach toward one Matthew Bower. "Why did he have to come to Key West, Lord? Isn't there another place he could set up his business?"

eight

Carmen greeted Peg with a curious stare. "What's the matter?"

"Matt Bower bought the property."

"Oh dear." Carmen put down the broom. Her wonderfully tanned complexion and dark black hair glistened in the tropical heat. "What are you going to do?"

"I don't know. I brought home the books and thought I'd see if I should even bother with a new storefront, or try and do piecemeal work from my apartment. I've certainly established a clientele."

"True." Carmen brightened. "That's a wonderful idea."

Peg continued toward her private entrance into the house. Her sister-in-law followed. "Peg, Daniel told me about tomorrow."

"What?"

"Shh, I love you. I wouldn't say a word to anyone."

But why would he tell her?

Because she's his wife, Peg reasoned. Not that it made her comfortable with the notion that one more person knew her past. In a matter of two weeks, two additional people knew. Peg hung her head in shame and closed her eyes, fighting back the raw emotions.

"If it's any consolation, I nagged him for the answer. Once he finally told me, I was ashamed that I had pushed him. I'm sorry, Peg. I promise no one will know from my lips."

Peg simply nodded her head. What could she say? Her nostrils flared; her breathing deepened. When she saw Daniel she would give him a piece of her mind. Not that it mattered any. He'd held her secret for twenty years. She supposed a good marriage was based on openness and honesty. But why did it have to be openness about her life?

Carmen placed her hand upon Peg's shoulder. "For what it's worth, I understand your pain. I lost a child at birth," she whispered.

Peg opened her eyes and looked into the dark brown eyes of her sister-in-law. She saw the sorrow, the understanding, the pain. Without another word, the two women embraced.

Carmen pulled back and wiped the tears from her eyes with a delicate handkerchief Peg had embroidered for her as a birthday gift. "You're welcome to spend the day with me tomorrow."

"Thanks, but I generally spend the day alone."

"*Sí.* I understand."

"Thank you."

Carmen left the apartment shortly after, and Peg changed into her casual clothing. She had the ledgers spread across the table, along with other scraps of paper, ready to work the figures. The question was should she take some time and walk the streets looking for vacant storefronts, then work on the books. A gentle knock on her door gave her a momentary reprieve from making the decision.

Daniel stood outside the door. His sandy brown hair shadowed his eyes. "Danny." Peg couldn't keep her hurt and anger from her voice.

"I'm sorry, Peg." Daniel hung his head.

"I can't believe you said anything. Why?" Peg placed her hands on her hips, blocking the entrance to her rooms.

"I don't know. May I come in? Please," he pleaded.

Peg stepped back and relaxed her hands at her sides.

"Thank you. I truly am sorry. I know I probably should never have said a word to Carmen. It's just so hard not telling her everything about me. I love her, Peg. She's such a part of me. I can't bear the thought of keeping things between us. And November twenty-eighth had come between us. I hope you don't hate me."

"No, I don't hate you. I'm disappointed, but I don't hate. How could I hate you, Daniel? Without you, I never would have made it those first couple of years."

Daniel cocked a half a grin up the right side of his face. "And you've been an equal blessing to me. I don't think staying in Savannah I would have grown as much. I would have followed in Father's footsteps and never been allowed to be myself, to follow my dreams, not his, you know?"

Peg grinned. "Yes, I know. It's hard to believe they are gone."

"I know. When I went home to settle their accounts, it was hard selling everything Father had worked so hard for. And yet, there was nothing there for you or me. I just wished we could have convinced them to move to Key West." Daniel sat down on the sofa.

"Me too." Her father had been a hard man. A man of the sea, who'd lived through more storms than he could count. To have him and their mother die from an accident on shore seemed so strange. They had managed to visit Key West a couple of times over the years, but their visits were far too few and far too short. On the other hand, Peg realized she could have gone home and visited also. But she could never face the folks back home. Her mother swore no one knew, but she didn't trust Billy and what he might have said before he left town.

"Peg, Carmen won't say anything."

"I know. It's a hard year, Daniel. I don't know why, but it is. Last year seemed so serene. I thought I was getting used to it. But this year. . ."

"What do you think is different?" Daniel folded his arms across is chest.

"Mother and Father being gone, I suppose."

"Hmm, I suppose that's possible. Oh, is it true that Matthew Bower bought your place?"

"Yup. Right out from under me."

"I'm sure he didn't buy it intentionally to hurt you."

Peg nibbled her lower lip. "Maybe not, but it sure feels that way. I brought the books home to go over them."

"Carmen said you might work from the house. Personally, I think that's a great idea. You don't have any extra financial needs. We've done well over the years. You could even retire, and you'd still be taken care of."

"We don't have that much money, Danny."

"Okay, I'd still have to work. But we've invested well. My biggest mistake was not buying Jefferson's property years ago. Then you wouldn't be in the place you're in right now."

Peg grinned. "At the time, Jefferson wanted far more than it was worth. I imagine he's come down a few dollars."

"Oh, I imagine so. Word is, Matthew Bower is quite a businessman. He's fair, honest, and he can barter with the best of 'em." Daniel grinned.

"He's a smooth talker, that's for sure." Peg rubbed the ever-growing stiffness in the back of her neck.

"And tell me, is the word on the street correct that you and he are engaged?"

"What?"

"Just fooling with ya. Nothing's been said for a week now. I think folks were hoping for a romance, but they've seen you're just not interested." Daniel eased himself deeper into the sofa.

"I've spouted off more Scripture verses from Paul talking about the nobleness of remaining single in the past couple of weeks. Folks ought to be getting the idea." Peg finally sat down on the overstuffed chair in her sitting room.

"What are your plans for tomorrow?" he asked.

"The same. I'll find a nice quiet beach and pour out my soul to God. I have a feeling I'll be doing a lot more pouring this year."

Daniel reached over and placed his hand around hers. "When are you going to forgive yourself?"

"I'm working on it. It's hard. I still can't shake the thought that if I hadn't sinned, my baby would have been alive."

"If you hadn't sinned there wouldn't have been a child and I doubt there ever would have been one with Billy. I don't think the man ever would have married you, and I don't think he would have made you a good husband if he had."

"Daniel, please. It wasn't just Billy's fault."

"I know that. But," he hesitated. "Peg, I heard some things about Billy when I returned home. He was hung for murder, Peg. He—"

"Murder?" Peg's breath caught in her throat.

"I double-checked. Apparently, he returned to Savannah back in 1850, just about two years after we left. Anyway, seems he got into a drunken brawl with someone. Before the dust cleared, Billy was standing over the man with a smoking pistol in his hand. He didn't deny killing the man. Word is, he never said he was sorry for it. He stood proud of himself and his actions in front of the hangman's noose."

"Don't you think if he and I had. . .waited, his life would have been different?" Peg felt tears sting her lids.

"I don't think so, Peg. There were other things I heard about Billy when you and he were engaged. Remember, we talked about those before."

And she did remember. But she never wanted to see how bad Billy really was. He'd always been sweet to her. Of course, his being sweet had caused her to sin. It was one of the things that kept her leery of smooth talkers. Smooth talkers like Matthew Bower.

No wonder she was fearful of the man. She realized she had kept Matt at a safe distance because he was like Billy, not in looks, but in his manner with women.

"Peg, it's been twenty years. You need to forgive yourself," Daniel whispered, breaking her thoughts.

"I know. I'm trying."

"Are you? Why take the day off? Why allow even one day to have a foothold over you?"

"I have to. It helps. It truly does allow me to be at peace the rest of the year. This year is just different."

"All right, Sis, I won't push you. I'll support you in any decision you make."

"Thanks. Now go home to your wife and children. I've got work to do."

"Yes, Ma'am." Daniel saluted.

"Hey, just remember, I'm the older sibling."

"Oh, like I could forget it, with you holding rank over me all these years," Daniel teased back.

She couldn't ask for a better brother. He'd supported her when no one else did, even her parents. Peg closed down the old images of anguish and pain her parents had levied against her all those many years ago. Tonight she had more important things to do. One of which included a quick walk through town to see what was and wasn't available for possible rent.

She left the house in her sandals, a light cotton skirt and blouse. She held her hair back with a leather barrette and a small stick. It was easier to manage this way and didn't take a lot of time to fashion.

The three-story buildings that lined Front Street were large, wooden clapboard structures scattered between homes and offices that belonged to lawyers and other businessmen. *When had the island changed so?* Peg wondered. Oh, she knew new businesses and buildings had gone up, but had she sheltered herself so much she'd become unaware of the changes on the island? Granted, all her free time was spent working or at church, and at work she stayed inside the store. Her chest heaved with the awareness that life was indeed passing her by.

"Peg? Peg Martin?"

Peg turned to the unfamiliar voice.

❧

"Mr. Bower, a pleasure to meet you. The island's been buzzing about this new business you're planning on starting here. Can't say I blame them. New industry is what we need here."

Matt had to grin at the older gentleman with white hair and a roughly shaved face. In the man's wrinkles, longer nubs remained from a less than close shave.

"Afraid I don't have any waterfront property for you," John Dixon grinned.

Matt smiled. "Not here for that. I bought Jefferson Scott's place this morning."

"You don't say. What will become of Peg Martin?"

Twist the knife deeper. "Well, Sir, that's why I'm here. William Horton mentioned you might have a place in your room facing Duval Street."

John scratched his scruffy chin. "Hmm, I suppose I do. What do you have in mind?"

"I was wondering if you might be willing to rent the place to Miss Martin. Seems a shame such a sweet little business like hers would need to go under just because I'm bringing in another."

"You don't sound like no sharp-nosed businessman I ever heard about." John gave him a sideways glance.

"That may be so, but I don't like the idea of making folks angry with me for no real reason. I had some time on my hands, and William did mention your place." There, he'd let the old gent gnaw on that for a bit.

"Makes sense. Well, I ain't been planning on renting the room, but iffin you wanna see it, I don't mind showing you."

Matt waited as John rose slowly from his chair. For an old man, he seemed pretty agile in spite of the gnarled hands and bent spine. Matt guessed the man to be close to eighty.

"These old bones slow down iffin I don't keep 'em moving." John led the way to a side room of his house. It had a private entrance and large bay windows on either side of the door. The room, a large rectangle, perhaps twenty feet wide and about fourteen feet deep, lay before him. It had a nice hardwood floor and plenty of room for Peg to put her shelves.

"What would you want to rent it for?"

"Can't say that I know. I don't need much, but I don't believe in giving something for nothing either. Do you know what she was paying Jefferson for his place?"

"Can't say that I do. Would you be willing to give her the same price?"

"Iffin Jefferson will verify that's the price he charged her, I don't see why not. I've just been using it for storage. The kids don't visit too much. Don't need a lot of space."

"How many children do you have?" *Pleasant conversation wouldn't hurt,* Matt thought.

"Five. I have seventeen grandchildren and half a dozen great-grandchildren, at last count. Most have moved to the mainland. My youngest daughter, she's in her fifties, she lives here on the island with her husband. Other than a handful here, the rest are spread out. I live for the letters. They all write me."

"That's wonderful. I have a son, and this is the first time I've spent any real time away from him. He attends the university, but he comes home on weekends and such."

"I remember my wife when the first ones moved away. She flopped around like a flounder."

"Micah didn't go to the university until after his mother passed away. We couldn't see giving her more pain."

"Sorry to hear you lost your wife. Hard to lose someone so close to you. Worst part was losing a child, though. Ain't natural, you know?"

"Right." Matt scanned the room again. "May I invite Miss Martin to come and pay you a visit?"

"She's welcome. Might be fun having folks coming and going all the time." John grinned. He hiked up his suspenders and led them back to the main part of his house.

Matt exchanged a firm handshake and headed back toward Peg Martin's home. He grinned, seeing how short of a distance she would have to walk each morning to go to work. Two and a half blocks.

He rapped on the door. Paused. No answer.

He knocked again. Paused. Again no answer. He turned down the pathway leading away from the house.

"Who are you?"

nine

Peg turned. How did she know this person? Or better yet, how did this person know her?

"Don't recognize me, huh?"

Dark chestnut hair turned up neatly in a bun framed her face. A thin nose, with a slight crook in the middle of it, set the woman apart from others.

"I'm afraid I don't."

"Must be 'cause I was around seven the last time you saw me."

Peg knitted her eyebrows. Who was this strange woman staring her down? "I'm sorry, but I don't recognize you."

"Not a problem. Jasmine Seymore."

Jasmine Seymore. Peg rolled the name around. It seemed somewhat familiar.

"I used to play with Elsie Beasley."

"Ah, I remember now." Elsie was the little girl she cared for when she first arrived on the island.

"How have you been?" Jasmine asked.

"Just fine. Yourself?"

"Good. The folks moved to Mobile when I was seven. This is my first trip back to the island."

"What brought you back?"

"Memories, mostly. My husband decided the best way to have me stop talking about this place was to bring me here for a visit. So here I am. Do you know what happened with Elsie?"

"She and her family moved to St. Augustine years ago."

"Oh." Jasmine was noticeably disappointed.

"Where are you staying?"

"A hotel down Front Street."

"Wonderful." Peg didn't want to seem rude, but the sun was setting. "I have a store, Southern Treasures, on the harbor. Come on over and visit sometime. I'm afraid I need to get going."

"Great, I'll try to come by your place." Jasmine waved good-bye and headed toward her hotel.

Twenty years and I see someone from way back then. Amazing! Lord, what are You trying to get me to realize here?" Peg hurried home, making a mental note of every possible store front. She couldn't believe how many places were vacant. Maybe she could afford renting some place else after all.

As she approached her house she heard her niece yell, "Who are you?" Peg picked up her pace. Mariella's tone conveyed caution. The island was basically a safe place, but she didn't want her niece in any danger.

She rounded the corner to see Matthew Bower holding his hands out to his sides, showing he wasn't a threat. Mariella, on the other hand, held a pole in her hands and was ready to swing. "Mariella, it's all right. He's a friend."

Mariella relaxed her aggressive stance. "He says he was looking for you."

"Yes, I imagine he is. You go on home now. I'm sure your mother must have dinner ready."

"All right. Sorry, Mister." Mariella tossed her weapon into the hedges that lined the front of the house.

"Sorry about that. I've never seen her so aggressive."

Matt chuckled. "No harm done. I'm glad you came home, though. I had some interesting news I wanted to share with you."

Hadn't he *shared* enough news today? "Come on in. I'll fetch you a glass of iced tea."

"Thanks. I could use something. I've been out in this heat most of the afternoon." Matt fanned himself with his hat.

Peg led him into her apartment. Having decided earlier why this man seemed such a threat to her, she felt she could guard against it. "Make yourself comfortable while I get us something to drink."

Matt nodded and chose the overstuffed chair. Which, she decided, was a noble thing, leaving the sofa and the rocker for herself to choose from. Billy would have chosen the sofa and encouraged her to sit beside him. She made quick work of their drinks and carried them out to the sitting room. "So, what brought you here this evening?"

He took the glass she offered him and gulped a healthy portion before answering. "I think I found a storefront for you."

"What?" She raised her voice in disbelief. *What is this man trying to prove?*

"I was placing an order with William Horton and we got to talking about Southern Treasures and how you'd have to relocate, and he mentioned John Dixon might have a room suitable for you."

"John? He doesn't have a storefront."

"Yes and no. He has a grand room on the side of his house that faces Duval Street. It has its own entrance and two bay windows on either side of the door. Actually, I think it's quite nice. It has more room than your present storefront, and it's not too far from your home."

"But it's so far out of town. One of the things that has helped my business prosper has been the sales from travelers who depart from the various ships. They spend some time in port and end up buying some trinkets for loved ones. No one would make their way up Duval Street just to buy something."

"I hadn't thought of that. I'm sorry. John said he'd rent the place at the same price you were paying Jefferson, if Jefferson would verify that's what you have been paying him."

Peg chuckled. "Sounds like John. He's a cautious old man. Wise though."

"I know I've sprung this on you, and I'm not trying to control your life or your decisions, but you might want to look at the place. It really has some potential. You may miss out on the tourist traffic, but from what I hear, the ladies of the island will be disappointed to see your store go. I feel badly for purchasing the building your store is located in, and I wanted to help."

"Would you consider selling your property?" Peg teased.

Matt's eyebrows rose and he clamped his mouth shut. Peg snickered at his expression. "Dan and I had considered buying the property years ago, but Jefferson was asking too much for it."

"Oh."

"I didn't know he was seriously considering selling the place until you mentioned it on our way back from the Southards' that evening. By then it was too late to put in a bid. Not to mention, it seemed somewhat unethical bidding on a piece of property you were going to bid on."

"That's just business. You should have." He reclined back in the chair.

"But if I had, you would have paid more."

"True." Matt sipped his tea. "Thanks for not bidding. It took some work to get the man down to a fair price."

"I imagine it did." Jefferson Scott could be one of the most stubborn individuals she'd ever known. But he'd been a good landlord and hadn't raised the rent on her over the entire seven years she had been there. Of course, he knew she wouldn't have been able to afford more rent and would have moved out. Which, in the end, would have caused him to lose even that small bit of income.

"There are a lot of vacant storefronts. I was out looking."

"Perhaps John Dixon's place isn't the answer for you then." Matt swirled the ice in his glass. "I haven't eaten this evening. Would you care to join the enemy for dinner tonight?"

"You're not my enemy, Matt."

"I'm glad to hear that, but the offer for dinner still stands. I'd love to have some company tonight."

He seemed almost melancholy, as if he were terribly lonely. Indeed, he appeared as she felt on this the eve of her son's birth and death. "You know, I think it would be nice to have dinner with you. I'm facing a mountain of book work and would love to put that off."

"Book work? I'm rather handy with figures. Could I help?"

"No, it isn't necessary. I'm just trying to decide what I can and cannot afford with regard to other rental options."

"I see. Well, if after dinner you'd like a hand, I'm more than happy to lend it."

"Thanks. Let me change, and I'll be right with you."

"Peg, you look fine. You don't need to go fancy yourself up. Our options for dinner establishments are limited."

"True. I suppose I could go in this." Peg stood and examined her skirt for wrinkles.

"We're simply going out as friends."

"Have you heard the recent gossip?" Peg teased.

"No, I don't believe I have. What's on the grapevine now?"

"Oh, something about us getting engaged. Of course, they have me engaged to Nate as well." Peg gathered their empty glasses and brought them into the kitchen.

"Hmm, definitely don't dress up then. We wouldn't want them having us married and on our honeymoon." Matt chuckled.

"You do understand small town gossip."

"Definitely. It was disturbing at first, but I think I'm reasonably comfortable with it now."

Peg chuckled.

⋙

She found she rather enjoyed Matt's presence. Whatever problems or tension that existed between them seemed to have diminished. Could the solution to her worries have been as easy as finally recognizing his likeness to Billy? She didn't want to give it any further thought right now. Instead, she found herself relaxing and enjoying Matt's stories about his son and wife.

"So, tell me what brought you to Key West?" Matt asked.

"Ah, well, a fresh start mostly. My father was a fisherman. A proud fisherman. Daniel enjoys the ocean, but he's never gotten used to the churning of the sea. He didn't want to follow in our father's footsteps, so we came here for a new start."

"Hmm. My father was the same way concerning the family business. I did go into it, but not until after I went away for my university training. Being forty-five, I now understand my father's desires. When I was eighteen, and full of myself and my own dreams, I didn't understand the man."

"I suppose some of that was true for Danny as well. He had a good mind for business, but Daddy didn't see that. He only saw honest pay for honest work. He wasn't too sure about investments and such. Thankfully, my father allowed us to leave."

Matt pushed back his chair from the table and folded his

hands across his stomach. "So, you left your home for your brother?"

"Somewhat. I had my reasons for wanting to live someplace else as well. But at least here Daniel could develop in business. And he has. He helped the wreckers market their sales, and we invested in some real estate. Nothing much, but it's been profitable."

"So, why did you open Southern Treasures?"

Peg eased back in her chair, rather pleased with how easily the words had fallen from her lips about their reasons for coming to Key West. Of course, she and Daniel had rehearsed them so many times. It wasn't like they were lying, since there was truth to the matter. It just wasn't the whole truth. "Probably because, as I've gotten older, simply making money wasn't as satisfying. With the embroidery I see a finished product. I see the joy it brings on people's faces. It's a more personal business. Does that make sense?"

"Yes, I understand that completely. My business is export. No faces, no personal connection. My personal connection comes with my employees. The work I do provides jobs for them and a real income for their families. If I'm lax, then I have to lay folks off. If I work hard, then they have a decent income throughout the entire year."

"Does it bother you that so many people are depending upon you?"

"Actually, no. At first, when I was a young man, it did. So many days I wanted to simply kick off my shoes and stay home with my family. But duty would nip at my conscience, and I'd kiss my wife good-bye and head for work, all the time wanting to be at home, relaxing and enjoying life."

"Didn't you take off a day or two a week?"

"Oh, sure. Sundays, of course. And an occasional Saturday.

But, more often than not, I ended up working some portion of that day. The hardest time was when my wife was dying. I hated to go to work, and yet I needed to for my own sanity, to think about something other than the pain Esther was enduring." Matt clamped his jaw tight and closed his eyes.

Without thinking, Peg reached over and placed her hand upon his forearm. "I'm sorry."

Matt's eyes shot open. The sudden movement made Peg jump and remove her hand. How could she have been so forward—so foolish?

⁂

Matt couldn't believe she had reached over and touched him. She knew the rumors that would buzz, but for a moment, he had allowed her tender touch to do exactly as she intended, sooth his weary soul. For two years, he had chastised himself for seeking relief from feeling his wife's pain.

Esther had understood his need to go to work, but she also wanted him next to her. She cherished his touch. It calmed her. He knew it. She knew it. But still he went to work faithfully every day. He was such a cad.

"I'm sorry," Peg whispered.

"No, it's all right. I was thinking of the gossips." *Good cover,* he mumbled to himself.

"I doubt it, but I'll let you have that to save face."

She has you pegged, old boy. He grinned. "Perhaps we best not talk about it."

"Perhaps." Peg dabbed her lips with the white linen napkin. "I think it is about time for me to be getting home, or I'll never get that paperwork done."

"I'd be more than willing to give you a hand."

"What, and incite the gossips all the more by coming late in the evening into my home?" She fanned herself like a proper Southern lady. "My dear Mr. Bower, what would people say?"

He held his hands up. "I surrender."

Peg grinned and acknowledged his assent with a single nod of her head. He escorted her home and left her.

What was he thinking, trying to take on this woman? *A woman so capable of deceit.* He thought back over the story she had told him. He could see the logic in Daniel Martin needing to find his own way in the world. But he knew the truth, the full truth. She hid it, and hid it well, he mused.

When he reached the small cottage he had recently secured for his dwelling, he was greeted with a letter tacked to the door. A letter from Micah. Matt ripped the sealing wax and rushed inside to light an oil lamp. Tomorrow was Micah's birthday, and he so much wanted to be with his son.

His son—how could he live with himself knowing Micah wasn't really his son? He had to get up the nerve to. . . No, it was best this way. To tell Micah would be to shatter his world. To tell Peg Martin would be to shatter her world. The best alternative was to keep the secret hidden. *Why had Dr. Baker found it necessary to tell the truth on his deathbed?* Matt raked his hands through his hair.

He needed to tell Peg. It simply wasn't fair to her. But how does a man go about saying, "You know that illegitimate child you had twenty years ago? Well, he's alive and well. Apparently, he didn't die at birth as the doctor had told you. Apparently, he switched the baby with another patient's dead infant. My wife's own dead child."

Who in the world would believe him? Doctors didn't do that. It was unethical.

But old Dr. Baker seemed to think it was ethical. Perhaps not, though, since he had needed to confess the truth before he met his maker.

"Lord, why did he have to tell me? Micah and I would have gone along just fine not knowing the truth. We would have continued our comfortable life. Now I'm faced with hiding the truth or exposing it. How do You think the people on this island would react knowing Peg Martin had an illegitimate son? That he'd been taken away from her at birth and given to another couple. It just doesn't seem fair."

Matt closed down his emotions and focused on the now crumpled letter in front of him.

Dear Dad,

I'm fine and looking forward to our time together in Key West. I still can't imagine why you are locating the business down there, but your reasoning always seems to make good business sense. The office here is holding up without you. I'm working when I'm not in classes. My final exams will put a strain on my ability to do well for the business.

I've met a charming young lady here in Savannah. She's a delightful creature, has the same blue eyes and wavy blond hair as myself. Her real father has a past the family would not be proud of. But, Father, her heart is as pure as any I've ever seen.

I suppose I sound like a love-sick puppy, but truthfully I'm not. I'm still praying about whether this is the woman the Lord has put in my path for love or for a mutual friendship. We met at a corner restaurant where I've been taking my meals. We have so many similar interests, and yet we have our differences. I don't know, Father. I am looking forward to discussing this matter with you when I reach Key West. Oh, before I forget, her name is Anna Ingles.

Thank you for the wonderful gift for my birthday, early of course. It's hard to believe we are apart on this day. Mother always made it such a special day for us. I still miss her terribly, but it's getting easier.

All my love, your son Micah

Matt's hands trembled. His heart pounded in his chest. His son was considering marriage. *Is he old enough for that? Am I old enough for that?*

ten

"November twenty-eighth." Peg groaned and pulled the pillow over her head. Sleeping the day away sounded good. She flipped her body around to the other side of her bed, closed her eyes, and prayed the day would just pass. All night she had dreamed about giving birth and hearing her son's first cry. His only cry. The doctor had pulled him out of the room before she had a chance to look at him.

Someone was pounding on her front door. Peg pulled the pillow off her head to be certain. Yup, someone was knocking. Peg plopped the pillow back over her head. Nope, she wasn't fit to deal with people today. The house could be burning down and she wouldn't move.

Peg paused, lifted the pillow just in case, and made certain there was no smell of smoke in the air. Sensing none, she groaned and pulled the pillow over her head once again.

Muffled sounds of someone calling her name between the heavy banging fluttered to her brain. Someone wanted her attention and wanted it badly.

"Nope. It's my day. I don't care who it is or why they've come, I'm not answering the door, Lord. Not today."

"Peg," a female voice called to her.

Peg lifted the pillow. The voice was far too clear. Had the person walked around her house to her bedroom window?

"Peg," the voice called again, but from the wrong direction.

She turned and faced her bedroom door.

"Bea?"

"It's about time you surfaced," Bea chided.

"What are you doing here?"

"I'm here about a friend, a dear friend."

"What?"

"You silly. You told me today was the day. . ." Bea let her words trail off.

Peg closed her eyes. "Me and my big mouth." She plopped the pillow over her face and rolled back under the covers.

"Hush now. I'm going to the kitchen and make us something to eat. Then we'll talk."

"Bea, honestly, go home. I prefer to be alone."

"I'm sure you do. It's been twenty years, Peg. And trust me, this will be the last time you will respond this way. Today is the day you deal with the past and forgive yourself once and for all." Bea left without waiting for a response.

How dare she come in here and assume she has the cure-all for what ails me. The nerve! Peg huffed. She threw the covers off, marched over to her robe, and put it on.

Stomping down the hallway, she made her way to the kitchen. "Just who do you think you are, Bea? You can't come into a person's house and tell them what they are going to do."

"Oh, so you like living like this? Going through this anguish every year?"

"No, but. . ."

"Exactly. Peg, sit down. Let me get us some tea, and we can discuss it." Bea turned and pulled open the cupboards, looking for the teacups.

"Where's James?"

"In your sitting room. He's fine for awhile. He ate well and fell asleep on our way over."

"Go home, Bea. I can handle this."

"Of course, you can. But this year you've got me to help you through it. You don't need to handle this alone. Tell me about being pregnant. Personally, I couldn't wait to give birth to James. This heat and those extra pounds were a killer."

"Thankfully I was in cooler weather for the last months," Peg answered without thinking.

"Did you name him? I mean, while you were expecting, did you call him anything?" Bea poured the water into the kettle.

Peg's voice caught. "Yes. I named him John, God's gift."

"No wonder it hurt so much when he died." Bea stepped up beside her. "I want you to tell me everything, Peg. Who his father was, how you fell in love. How it felt to lose your very heart and soul once he was born. Everything. We'll get you through this, and you'll be able to accept the past, your flaws, and God's grace."

"I don't know, Bea. I pour my heart out to God every year. It's no use."

"Ah, but this year you have me to hear you, to sympathize with you, and to tell you where you're missing the mark."

Peg chuckled. "You're rather sure of yourself."

"Hey, I've been living with Cook for a couple years now. Something has had to wear off on me." Bea grinned.

Peg tossed her head from side to side. Maybe she should try it Bea's way. After all these years, her way wasn't working. "I'll try, Bea. But if I need space you have to promise me to give it to me."

"Fair enough. So, start from the beginning. How'd you meet John's father?"

Peg began slowly to tell Bea about her whirlwind romance with Billy. How handsome he was. How persuasive.

The day wore on. James was a perfect child, eating and

sleeping while they talked.

"Billy just ran away, huh?"

"Yes. Daniel says he was in some other trouble. At the time I didn't want to listen. I was so certain he left because I told him I was with child, that we would have to get married right away."

"That could make a man run. On the other hand, he seemed to speak from both sides of his mouth, talking about his great love for you and then running away from you. Seems to me there might be something to what Daniel said he heard about him."

"I think you're right. Daniel told me yesterday that when he went home last year to settle Mother and Father's estate after they died that word was Billy had returned a couple years later only to stir up more trouble. Seems he killed a man and hung for it."

"Oh my," Bea gasped.

"Isn't a pretty image, is it? What's worse is that Danny said he showed no remorse for anything he'd done, knowing he was about to die. He stood there, proud as a peacock."

"Lord, have mercy. How can a man be so hard?"

"I don't know. I don't recall much of that Billy. He only showed me that side of himself the night I told him about John."

Bea reached out and took Peg's hand.

"Did your parents ever soften?"

"Eventually they saw I changed. Mother said she used to place flowers on John's grave. They really did forgive me."

"Then you can forgive yourself, Peg. Face it, you're human, and we humans make mistakes. Lots of them. Some are big, and some are not so big. Some we can hide and keep in secret. Others show themselves in time. Thankfully, we have a Savior who died for those sins and covers them with His blood."

"I know God forgives. I suppose I know I should forgive myself."

"Of course, you know it. The question is, are you strong enough to release yourself from the guilt, to allow God's grace to perform a miracle in your life? To accept a gift for the future?"

"What gift?"

"Oh, I don't know. A husband, perhaps?"

"Not you too?"

"*Moi?* Surely you jest." Bea feigned a hand to her chest.

Peg rolled her eyes.

"Seriously, Peg. I don't know if there is or isn't a man in your future. I'm just saying, being bound to the past can't allow you to go forward. You're limiting what God can and wants to do through you. You, more than anyone, know there are many who have gone through what you have. Those women could use a gentle hand, a kind word, to help them come to our heavenly Father. And someone who's been through it, like yourself, can help."

Peg thought of Julie in New York and how she was able to help Nate understand what had happened to her. Julie's most recent letter to Nate confessed the rape, how much shame she felt, and how her family tried to help her. And yet, somehow they weren't sure she did everything possible to prevent the rape from happening. Nate had run off to New York on the next ship heading north. *Maybe Bea's right, Lord. Maybe I can be of help to some women.*

"Peg, you know Grace Perez, right?"

Peg nodded.

"Well, she's expecting. It's all hush-hush, but one of my husband's employees is the father. He ran off to Cuba as soon as he found out. She's scared, and she's alone."

"But. . ." If she started helping folks, her own shame would be known. Hadn't she and Daniel left Savannah so they wouldn't have to live in shame?

"I'm not telling you to do or say anything. I'm just pointing out there are people who could use the wise words of someone like you."

"Wise? You can't be serious. I still feel like a flounder flopping on the deck of a ship. I even have dreams that my son is alive and well."

"Well, that's just your mother's heart having a hard time accepting the loss. I don't know if you'll ever get over that."

"No, I suppose you're right. I don't think I'll ever get over it."

"Did you see him after he was born?"

"No. The doctor just whisked him off to another room, then came back in and told me."

Bea closed her eyes, then opened them slowly. "That doctor deserves a good swift kick in the backside. Who did he think he was, telling you it was all your fault for having relations outside of marriage? I swear, he cursed you."

"Cursed me?"

"I guess that's the wrong word. But it seems to me that those words of his are the ones that have rambled around in your head for all these twenty years. The words that haven't allowed you to forgive yourself. You know as well as I that God doesn't kill every child that is conceived out of wedlock. In fact, He's taken sinners and those who are the result of sin and included them in His own heritage. Look at Rahab, the harlot. Who would have thought God would have used her to be a great-great-great-grandmother to Jesus? Well, more than three greats back—many greats—but you get my meaning."

Peg rubbed her hands over her face. Had she let the doctor's words bind her to the past? Was that why she couldn't forgive herself? Was it his unkind words that brought judgment and self-condemnation?

"I see I've got you pondering."

Peg groaned.

"Tell me, is the word on the street true? Are you and Matthew Bower seeing each other socially?"

❧

Matt pushed down his inner thoughts today. He would not visit Peg Martin. As curious as he was to see her, and see how she was handling the past, he knew he didn't want to see her in anguish. He didn't want to see eyes painted red from salty tears. No, she closed the store for a reason, and that reason was alive and well and living in Savannah. How much longer could he keep the secret? *Should* he keep it?

"Stop it, Bower. Enough is enough," he barked at the half-shaven face in the bathroom mirror. His straightedge razor slid down the left side of his jaw with ease. He'd tried growing a beard years ago, but found it was just as much work, if not more, to keep a beard groomed properly as it was to shave every morning. Besides, Esther always enjoyed his clean-shaven look. A slight grin made the lather rise on his cheek. He finished shaving and dressed for the day.

He had several meetings before him this morning. First, he'd need to find an architect to decide if tearing down the present building and restarting from scratch was a better option. He felt confident that tearing down the present structure was his only real choice, since sections of the dock were rotting, but he'd be prudent to examine the various possibilities.

He placed his reply letter to Micah in his pocket. Hopefully there would be a ship heading north that would be entering the

Savannah River before going further. Matt thought back on Micah's letter and a certain Miss Anna. He wondered what she was like, what his son found so compelling about her. Was she the one the good Lord had designed to be the perfect helpmate for Micah?

Matt knew he had a multitude of questions. He could hardly wait for his son's arrival as he worked his way down the ground coral streets.

"Good morning, Mr. Hewitt, how are you this morning?" he said as he entered an office building.

"Fine, fine. I heard you bought Jefferson Scott's place." The balding middle-aged man extended his hand.

"You heard right. I also was told that you might be the man to help me expand the dock and possibly the building." Matt stepped further into the man's office.

Hewitt's grin broadened. "I heard you got William Horton working on it."

"True, but I'm a businessman, and I expect bids. William will give me his by the end of the week. Are you interested?"

"Does a turtle have a shell?"

Matt chuckled. "Great." He went on to explain the specifications he had in mind for the work, then left Hewitt to his own devices.

So far, William Horton seemed to be the better man. His work spoke for itself. However, Matt knew business demanded estimates, and he'd be foolish not to look at every one.

Now to speak with Ellis Southard about shipping schedules. Matt headed toward Ellis's dock. He found Ellis and Mo working on the new building at the landside edge of his dock. "Morning, gentlemen."

"Morning," Ellis called down from the slight peak of a roof.

"I was wondering if I could have a word with you about

the shipping of your product."

"Sure, give me a minute to secure this beam." Ellis pounded the nails into the carrying beam, then climbed down the ladder. "What kinds of questions do you have?"

"I'm wondering if you have an exclusive contract with the various ships that come to port?"

"Not really. I've gotten to know several of the captains, and when they have extra space I'm able to place some of my wares on the vessel. Most of the time this works well, since sponges don't take up weight and can be wedged into many nooks and crannies onboard a ship."

"I see. Would you be interested in working out a schedule with my ships?"

"You own your own vessels?"

"Yes, Sir. I found it to be profitable in the long run. At first there wasn't much profit. But once I paid off the debt on the vessels, they soon paid for themselves."

"Interesting. I'd been thinking about purchasing my own ship for that very reason. We'll have to talk more."

eleven

The next week Matt found himself driven to see Peg Martin.
Thoughts of her and her suffering were beginning to plague
him. He knew the truth; she would no longer suffer once she
knew. But then again, it was always possible she'd suffer
even more knowing the last twenty years had been robbed
from her. Unable to determine what was best, he decided that
the only course of action was to befriend her, get a feel for
how she really thought. Then he could determine whether it
was best to keep the secret or to tell her. Micah would be
arriving in a matter of weeks. Matt had to settle this issue
before his son arrived.

"Good morning, Peg." He smiled upon entering her store.
"How are you?"

"Fine. Thought I'd seen the last of you. You know I keep men
at a distance, but you're something else. All I did was place my
hand upon yours at a point in which you had shared your heart
about your wife. I certainly wasn't interested in something
more, as you so obviously insinuated from the touch."

What was she talking about? The moment in the restaurant
flew back into his mind. "A simple touch was not the problem. Forgive me for giving you that impression."

"Seems to me you've been avoiding me."

"I reckon there might be some truth to that, but it wasn't
because you reached out and placed your hand upon my
forearm."

"The rumors?" Peg inquired.

"In part. Heard we were engaged and planning to have a handful of children. Personally, I'm not sure I'm young enough to have more children." He smiled.

"Children? Just how many are we supposed to have?" Peg flowed right in with the gentle teasing.

"Last count, I think we were up to three."

"Three's not too bad. But a woman my age. . .and running around after young'uns. . .I don't know. We might have to curb that rumor."

"How?"

"Oh, I don't know. Let's adopt some pets or something. Children take a lot of time."

She's not too interested in having children, Matt mused. How would she have been as the mother of Micah?

"On second thought, let's have a baker's dozen. I mean, if were going to have them, we might as well go all out," she teased.

"Thirteen? Woman, you'd bury me in an early grave."

"Ah, but just think how many wonderful memories I'd have of you by looking into the delightful faces of your children." She winked.

Matt's stomach fluttered. He swallowed hard. Perhaps this game of one-upping the local gossips wasn't really such a good idea. "Have mercy, dear lady. I have only fathered one. I'm ill prepared for a house full of little ones under foot."

Peg chuckled. "You know, I don't know if I could handle a pack of young'uns. I love children. Don't get me wrong. But I'm old enough now where I like things quiet and simple."

Matt smiled. "Trust me, I understand. When my younger sister brings her children over to the house for a visit, it takes all the patience I can muster. I was spoiled having only a single child, I suspect."

Peg looked down to the floor. *Oh, that was brilliant,* he chided himself. She obviously loved children. So why had she not gotten married after she had her child and had some more? She had admitted keeping men at a distance. *Has she not made peace with the past? Is that why she takes the day off on Micah's birthday?*

"Seriously, I've been rather busy getting some bids and working out the time schedules for relocating the business. I'm thinking I might keep a smaller operation going in Savannah. But I'm not sure I could handle the two locations. Micah's been working hard trying to keep things running, but I'm uncertain whether he'll want to stay in Savannah or come and work here with me."

"Ah, you're like my father, deciding for your son what his future should be."

"No. Micah's gone to the university. He's doing what he wants."

"Is he? Have you given him the options or have you just assumed?"

Had he given Micah the option? Had he listened to the desires of his son's heart and not just assumed he would want to follow in his father's footsteps with the family business? Matt sighed. "I believe I gave him the choice."

"What does he love?"

Matt stepped up to the counter. "At the moment he seems fascinated with a young lady." Matt chuckled.

"Oh, do tell."

"Apparently she works at a restaurant he's been taking his meals at. He says her father has a past the family might not be pleased with."

"Ooh, a touch of scandal for Savannah. I like that," Peg teased.

"I'm not so concerned about the young lady's father as much as I am concerned about whether or not she loves Micah. But he is aware of how certain women are attracted to him because of his family wealth. Ever since he was sixteen, he's had certain women swooning at his feet. He's a handsome young man, which makes him a very desirable catch."

"If he looks as fine as his father, I'm certain the ladies find him irresistible."

Is she flirting with me?

"Now don't read something into what I just said," she said quickly, as though reading his thoughts. "I was merely commenting on your handsome features. A woman notices a handsome man, you know. We just aren't like the men who hoot and holler when a fine specimen walks past."

Matt roared. "My dear Peg, in my neighborhood a man does not hoot and holler over a woman. He simply takes an appraising glance at her fine assets."

Peg broke out in a hearty laugh.

⋙

Tears of laughter poured down Peg's face. It was good to laugh, to enjoy life. And she had to admit it, Matthew Bower brought humor and joy back into her life.

Matt collapsed on the stool in front of the counter. Their game of tempting the gossips was really quite fun. He pulled out a white handkerchief and handed it to her.

Peg retrieved it and dabbed the tears from her eyes and cheek. His musky scent on the handkerchief filled her nostrils. A flutter of awareness that she was drawn to this man in a way she'd not been drawn to another in so many years coursed through her veins like a riptide. "We shouldn't tease the gossips."

"But it's so much fun," Matt snickered.

"True, but how many do you suppose might take our teasing humor and run with it?"

"Let 'em run. You and I know the truth. That's all that should matter."

"I suppose you're right, and it is fun playing like this. I don't know when I've laughed this hard in years."

"Me, either. I guess Esther's death took a part of myself."

Peg sobered. "I would imagine it would. You said you'd been married for twenty years, and you said you had a good marriage."

"Yes. We had a good marriage."

Peg stepped back behind the counter and pulled her needlework out from behind it.

"What are you working on now?" He asked.

"Oh, something for a special family member."

"May I see?" Matt reached out.

Peg held it up for him.

"John, God's gift," Matt read.

"It's a pillow."

"You really have quite a talent there. Names can be so powerful. Micah means 'who is like the Lord.' "

She smiled, her eyes on her work. Since the twenty-eighth, she had felt the burden lifted from her shoulders. Bea was right, that day had marked the end of her sorrow. It had been time to forgive herself. Actually, she should have forgiven herself years ago but. . .what did it matter? It was done. She was at peace with the past.

"As much as I enjoy your fine company, I must get back to work. Would you be free this evening to join me for dinner?" Matt stood, his eyes fixed on her for an answer.

"What, and have them up the number of children we'll have to four?" Peg teased.

Matt raised his hands. "Don't start that again. I'll not be able to keep a straight face when I meet some of the folks on the street."

"Trust me, you're going to have a hard time with it anyway. I'll be happy to join you tonight, though. But how about if I fix us up something special? Could you use a home-cooked meal?"

"Woman, don't tempt me." Matt grinned. His green eyes sparkled with excitement. Maybe inviting him to her house wasn't such a good idea, she realized. "If you're offering a home-cooked meal, how could a man turn that down? When should I arrive?"

"Better make it six. I don't close the shop until five."

"Sounds wonderful. Can I bring some fresh bread or rolls from the bakery?"

"That would be fine."

Matt nodded and proceeded toward the door. "Thanks, Peg. You're a breath of fresh air."

"So are you, Friend." Peg waved him off. Perhaps they could be just friends. Not all men and women had to get romantically involved in order to have a relationship, right? She rehearsed the morning conversation through her mind once again. What would it be like to have a child with such a handsome man?

"Child?" Peg groaned. She didn't even want to entertain that thought.

"Miss Martin?" A slender Hispanic girl stood in her doorway.

"Hello, Grace. Come in." Peg started to shake. Could she go through with this?

❧

Matt continued to chuckle as he walked toward the center of the business district. The town was relatively quiet this morning. People hard at work, he presumed. He marched over to the baker's and ordered a loaf of rye with raisins and chopped walnuts.

"I can make that. But you might have to buy the second loaf. Ain't a normal order down here." The baker stood with a white apron decorated with patches of flour and crumbs.

"I understand."

"I'll try and sell it to another customer but. . ."

Matt raised his hand. "No bother. I just haven't had that bread for awhile. I'm willing to pay for both loaves."

"You said you like it the way the French cook it?" The baker raised his furry gray eyebrows.

"Yes, is that a problem?"

"No, no. It's a hard crust. Simple, really. You just brush on some water to the outside of the bread before it cooks. Do you want a thick crust or thin, hard crust?"

"Thin, if you don't mind."

The baker grinned. "No problem. I can make it. You come by my store later. I'll fix you your bread. You see, Mario can bake anything."

"I'm sure you can. Thank you."

"You're welcome, Mr. Bower."

Matt supposed everyone knew his name, but he was certain he didn't know Mario's—other than the fact that the outside sign to the bakery shop said "Mario the baker." And he sounded Italian, which seemed odd. "I'm afraid I don't know your name, Mr.—"

"Mario Falluchi."

"Pleasure to meet you, Mr. Falluchi."

"Call me Mario. Everyone does."

Matt nodded his head. "Mario it is then. When should I come back?"

Mario glanced up at the wall clock. "Four o'clock."

"Perfect, I'll see you then." Matt stepped out into the balmy tropical sun. He really needed to get some cooler clothing if he was going to make his home here. He walked over to a small shop where men's attire hung in the front window. In between the baker's and this shop, he counted at least three vacant storefronts. Perhaps Peg was right; finding a place to rent wasn't going to be a problem for her.

"May I help you?" A short, well-rounded Hispanic woman came from the back room upon his entrance.

"I was looking for something a bit more comfortable in this heat."

"*Sí*, you need a Guayoubera"

"What's a Guayoubera?"

"A Cuban male's shirt. It's light and gives a man relief. You don't tuck it into your trousers like you wear your business shirts."

"Could you show me one?"

The friendly woman walked over to a row of shirts and pulled a white, short-sleeved boat of a shirt off the rack. He would have to be out of his mind to dress in that.

"Come, try it on."

"I—"

"*Señor,* try. If you don't like, no problem."

Matt removed his vest, tie, and then his dress shirt.

"*Hijo!* No wonder you're so uncomfortable."

Matt tried the strange shirt. He'd seen a few men dressed in these around the island. Even businessmen wore them in their offices. A tie was totally inappropriate for such a shirt. Perhaps he could adjust to them. They appeared comfortable.

"The shirt, it blocks the sun, but it's loose so the body heat can escape, *sí*?"

"Hmm, are they supposed to hang so loosely over the shoulders?" Matt lifted the shirt on the top of the shoulders and let it drop back down.

"*Sí.*"

"*Gracías.* How much?"

"Five dollars."

"Five dollars?" *How could a simple shirt cost so much?*

"Four?"

Hmm, he'd forgotten that some folks liked to barter and work their way down in price. He scanned the store and decided not to press the woman further. It seemed full of items and few customers. "I'll take five shirts then."

"*Gracías*, Mr. Bower."

Her eyes sparkled. He examined the shirt more closely. It was well tailored, and he suspected the saleswoman had made it. "Did you make these?"

"*Sí.* Do you want all white?"

"Let's add a little color—that light blue and pale yellow—the rest will be fine in white."

"No problem." She hesitated, then asked, "Do you need anything else?"

"Can you give me another Guayoubera in a smaller size, one for my son. His shoulders are not as broad as mine."

"*Sí*, I have just the Guayoubera for a young man."

She pulled another off the rack. It looked identical to the one he had on. "Thank you. It will make a fine Christmas present."

She nodded. Her smile stretched across her face and touched her eyes. Times had been tough on this island. Perhaps his company would help bring some welcome relief. The question was, how could he turn down an applicant? More would apply than he had jobs for. Matt sighed. *I guess I'll deal with that when the time comes, Lord.*

He paid for his Guayouberas and brought them to the small cottage. At home, he fixed a light lunch for himself and determined his afternoon schedule. A trip to Mobile to check on shipping from there might have to be planned soon. His recent letters had come back unanswered. His business depended on the farmers being able to ship their cotton to him as well. He penned another letter and prayed this one would be answered.

A rap at his door made him slip with his pen.

"Mr. Bower, come quick!"

twelve

Peg groaned. The gentle lull of the waves lapping the pilings confused her anguished mind. The throbbing pain made her open her eyes once again. She needed to focus.

"The pain!" she cried out.

"Hang on, Miz Martin. Help is on the way."

Who called to her? Where was she? Her fingers grasped the wooden planks around her. She tried to move her right leg.

A cry of pain ripped through her throat. "Oh, God, help me."

"Relax, Miss Martin. You're going to be all right."

Peg tried to focus. Who had spoken?

"Miz Martin, relax. I'll take care of you." Mo's familiar voice called out to her. Someone she recognized. At least a voice she recognized. When she opened her eyes, she saw several figures with no definite shape or size. Mo, on the other hand, was a large man. She figured he was the dark blob kneeling down in front of her.

Peg moaned.

"Give us some space!" called another voice she thought belonged to Ellis Southard. "Relax, Peg, Mo and I will get you out of here."

Out of where? Where was she? And why did it hurt so much? Why was she half standing, half lying face down. Wooden splinters bit into her cheek.

"Everyone move back. There's no telling how rotten some of these other boards are," Ellis ordered.

Peg heard various gasps from the crowd.

Water splashed below her.

"She's bleedin' bad. We've got to get her out, Mr. Ellis." Mo now lay beside her. "I can see below. She's pinned by a two-by-six that's cut into her right thigh."

Peg now understood. She'd fallen through a piece of rotten decking on the dock behind her store. She'd gone out there with Grace Perez to talk about private matters. Parts of that dock were unstable. She knew better. Peg mumbled, "I mustn't have been paying attention."

"Doc's on his way," someone yelled from some place off to her left.

Tears burned down her cheeks. "Oh, God, please help."

"Can you lift your body, Peg?" Ellis asked.

Peg pushed the boards with her hands. The pain increased. She screamed.

"Miz Martin, listen to me. I'm goin' to lift this here board, and Mr. Ellis, he'll pull ye out. Iffin you feel too much pain, grab my arm. We'll stop. All right?"

Peg nodded and placed her hand on Mo's large muscular forearm.

Words were mumbled. She felt Ellis reach his arms under her own. "Hang on, Peg."

Mo lifted.

"Stop!" she screamed clawing her nails into Mo's arm.

"Get me a saw!" Mo hollered.

"And some clean rags," Ellis added.

"I'm gonna cut the board, then when we lift it off you, it won't be pressing in on ye," Mo advised.

Peg licked her lips. Her stomach heaved. She closed her eyes and fought the onslaught of fresh pain. She couldn't feel her leg below the board in her thigh.

"What happened?" Matt gasped. "Get her out of there," he demanded.

"We're working on it," Ellis groaned.

Matt lay down on the boards beside Peg opposite Mo. "Hang on, Peg."

"I'm trying," she groaned through her teeth.

Matt reached in below the boards and held her thigh. She'd seen a flash of white linens in his hand but didn't dare ask where it came from. The pressure added slightly to her discomfort at first, then seemed to be helping.

Peg heard the sawing of the wood. With each thrust the board jiggled in her leg. "Oh, God, help!"

"Almost through, Miz Martin," Mo announced.

Almost wasn't good enough. She wanted him to stop, and she wanted him to stop *now*. The wood cracked beneath her, and she started to slide down. Another strangled scream tore its way passed her lips. "Dear Jesus, this hurts. Please help me, Lord," she cried.

"Clean rags," Matt demanded. He lifted his hand off her thigh and tossed the now bloodstained rags aside. "Now, Mo."

Mo pulled the board free from her leg. Ellis held on to her as she felt her body hang below the dock. Mo helped lift her as Matt continued to press the linens against her thigh.

"Bring her to my office. I'll need to operate," Doc Hansen ordered.

Peg blinked at the crowd. Blurred images of people standing there with horror on their faces slowly focused. Mo cradled her in his arms. Matt continued to press the rags on her thigh.

"Peg!" Daniel cried.

"Daniel," she whispered.

"She's goin' to be all right, Mr. Daniel. I need to take her to the doctor's office." Mo continued to hustle her in that direction.

"What happened?" Daniel asked.

Someone filled him in, or at least she thought she heard someone mumbling something about rotten boards. Her body chilled and heated at the same moment. She floated away from the pain, away from Mo's arms, into the deep recesses of her mind.

☙

Matt paced the length of Doctor Hanson's front parlor. Daniel sat in a chair, huddled over in prayer. Ellis and Mo left, with stern words to fetch them when there was news. They insisted on going down to the dock to repair the damage in case small children would be curious. Matt had to agree with them on that score.

Dark woodwork framed white plaster walls. Various pieces of Queen Anne furniture were neatly placed around the room. Every few minutes, someone would pop into the doctor's parlor and ask how Peg was doing. Did she have any idea how many people genuinely cared for her? Matt wondered.

"Mr. Bower, please sit down," Daniel pleaded. "Your pacing is making me more nervous."

"Sorry." Matt plopped down on the nearest chair.

"Do you think she'll be able to walk again?" Daniel asked, without really looking for an answer.

"I couldn't say. I pray she will."

"What was she doing back there on that dock anyway?" Daniel clutched his fist.

"I'm sorry. I was at home when it happened. I—I. . ." Matt mumbled.

"I'm sorry. I know you don't have the answers. I guess no one does but Peg." Daniel closed his eyes. "Lord, she has to be all right."

Matt heard Daniel's voice crack. He swallowed his own

bitter tears. *It's my dock. I'm responsible. I saw the condition of some of the wood. I should have roped it off. I should have done something, Lord.* Hindsight was always perfect. Matt folded his hands and kneaded the tension out of them.

He removed his pocket watch for the hundredth time. It had been three hours since he helped lay Peg's motionless body on the table.

The dark oak door creaked as it opened. Dr. Hansen dried his hands off with a fresh white towel. Blood stained his apron. Matt's stomach rolled. There was so much blood.

"Daniel," the doctor called.

Daniel's head popped up from prayer. "How is she, Doc?"

"She lost a lot of blood, but she's going to be fine. I want her to spend the night here, possibly another. It all depends on how quickly she responds."

Daniel nodded his head. "Whatever it takes."

"How badly was her leg injured?" Matt asked.

"There's a lot of damage to the quadraceps muscle. With God's grace, she won't lose her limb. But it will take some time before she can use it. We have to monitor the limb, watch for any signs of gangrene. I might have to remove it in order to save her life."

"No," Daniel gasped.

"What can we do to help prevent that?" Matt stepped closer to the doctor. There had to be something he could do.

"Change the dressing regularly. Message the limb, encourage the blood to flow back and forth in the limb."

Matt held his tongue. These were private matters for family, and he wasn't family. He'd only been raising her son for the past twenty years.

"I'll see to her care, Doctor." Daniel raised his shoulders and strengthened his resolve.

"Gentlemen, if you'll excuse me I have a patient to attend to." Doc Hansen stepped back toward his inner office. "Daniel, might I suggest you find a couple of women to take care of her. She'll need around the clock attention for a few days."

Daniel's face flamed as brightly as Matt's felt. "Yes, Sir," they mumbled in unison.

"Now go home and let me care for my patient. I don't have time for dealing with brothers and lovers."

"Lovers?" Matt and Daniel harmonized, looking at each other. "What?"

"You heard me. Now shoo, the both of you."

"Can I see her?" Daniel asked.

"No, I've not cleaned up in there, and I don't need another patient passing out on me. The nurse and I will have things cleaned up, and Peg should be awake by morning. Good day, gentlemen."

The doctor stepped back into his office, not waiting for a response.

"I'll see you in the morning, Daniel." Matt took a single step toward the door.

"No, Sir. You're going to tell me what's going on with you and my sister," Daniel demanded, his right hand fisted.

"Nothing, Daniel. Peg and I are friends. We haven't so much as even held hands. It's just this island and its silly rumors. In fact, Peg and I were joking about it this morning. Apparently, according to the gossip, we're engaged and going to have three children." Matt smiled.

Daniel relaxed his fist. "On your honor, it isn't true?"

"I swear. We're just friends."

Daniel nodded and made his way through the front door.

Matt sighed. *Of all the times to have to deal with small-town gossip, now is not it.*

Matt walked back to Southern Treasures and examined the repair job Mo and Ellis had done. The walkway was boarded off and a small sign read UNSAFE. He went to the door of the store and found it open. On the counter, folks had placed notes of get-well wishes and prayers. Matt grinned. *There are certain advantages to living in small towns,* he mused.

⁂

Peg groaned, her mind foggy. Pain coursed through her body. She blinked. The room seemed dark, her bed stiff. Opening her eyes, she tried to focus on something in the room, but everything seemed out of place.

She closed her heavy lids again and tried to think. She fought to reopen her eyes again. Her lids were unresponsive. A dark room means nighttime, she reasoned. *I'll just go back to sleep.*

"Miss Martin, how are you feeling?"

Peg grasped the edges of her bed. *Who was in her room?* Fear gave her eyelids the strength she needed. She shot them open. The room appeared brighter. Everything was not as it should be. "Where am I?"

"Relax, Miss Martin, you're at Doc Hansen's house."

Peg groaned. Memories of the accident, the pain, all flooded back. It all made sense now. She tried to bring into focus the darkened silhouette of the woman now sitting beside her. Peg smiled as Mary Hansen leaned closer to the light. The doctor's wife often worked side by side with her husband. She was his nurse, secretary, and anything else that needed doing in the office. "Mrs. Hansen."

"Yes, Dear. You've given us quite a scare. How are you?"

"Hot and sore. What happened to me?" Peg tried to roll onto her right side to face Mary. Pain surged anew up her right leg to her lungs. A cry of pain eased past her lips.

"Stay still, Peg. You don't want to undo my husband's fine

work." Gray wisps of Mary's hair fell out of her bonnet.

Peg glanced under the sheet toward her right leg. It seemed to be braced with something.

"You fell through the dock."

"Yes, I can remember that. But what damage did I do?"

"A board pierced your right thigh. There was damage to your leg muscles. You've been in and out for a couple of days due to a high fever brought on by infection, although my husband did give you something for the pain, which aided your sleep."

"A couple days?" Peg whispered. "What about my store? Christmas is only a few weeks away."

"I believe Mr. Bower has been taking care of your store. Your brother has been checking in as often as possible. In fact, half the island's been in here. Greg finally put a message on the slate informing them of your condition." Mary smiled. "My husband, as fine a doctor as he is, doesn't like answering the same question over and over again."

Peg relaxed against the bed. *Matt Bower is working in my store? Why?* "Two days?"

"Yes, Dear. Let me check your fever?"

"What time is it?" Peg asked when Mary took the thermometer from her mouth.

"Close to midnight. I'm not certain." Mary lifted the sheet over Peg's right leg.

Peg looked down and saw the swelling and discoloration. "Will it heal?"

"We hope so. You're fighting the infection well."

"Will—will, I have to lose my leg if the infection doesn't heal?"

"Oh, Peg, don't go frettin' about things before it's time. One thing is certain with medicine, no one knows too much before it happens. Some folks have lost their limbs from less of an injury, others have lost use of them, and still others recover quite well, and you'd never know they had been hurt. Just do as you're told, and I'm certain the good Lord will take care of the rest."

Was that supposed to encourage me? Peg wondered. *I could lose my leg, I could be lame, or I might possibly walk again. Oh, joy.* She bit down her sarcastic thoughts.

Mary glanced at her face. "I'm sorry, Peg. I should have kept my mouth shut. Relax. You're healing well. Can you see this?" Mary pointed to the outer side of Peg's right leg.

Peg lifted herself up on her elbows. "A little."

"Well, yesterday that area was bright pink. Today it's half the shade, much paler. A very good sign."

"Really?"

"Yes. I forget some folks don't want, or even need, to know all the possible problems they could be facing."

"No, don't apologize. I think I prefer knowing." Peg collapsed back on the bed. It was too difficult to hold herself up on her elbows. "I feel dizzy."

"You lost a lot of blood. But you're young, healthy."

"I'm not that young."

Mary grinned. "When you reach my age, you'll remember just how young thirty-eight is."

Peg chuckled. Her ribs hurt. "My sides hurt when I laugh."

"You cracked a rib. Not much the doctor can do but bind it. It shouldn't give you too much trouble."

Peg lay there wondering how many other injuries she sustained from her fall.

"Grace Perez has been coming by checking on you. She even sat for a spell, giving Greg and me some time to rest."

Peg nodded. Their private conversation had barely begun

when she fell through the dock.

Mary continued to change the bandages.

"Rumor has it that you and Mr. Bower are planning on getting married after his son arrives." Mary sat back down into her rocking chair.

Peg rolled her eyes and groaned. This time it wasn't from the pain.

"Another island legend, I see." Mary winked.

"Yes," Peg whispered.

"Normally, I'm not one to give ear to such conversation, but with the way he's been checking in on you and filling in at your store. . .I just thought it might be true." Mary picked up a small needlepoint.

"Matt probably feels somehow responsible for the accident since he bought the place. He isn't. It wasn't his fault. I knew better. I shouldn't have been out there."

"Why did you go out there?"

"Grace and I had some private matters to discuss. I didn't want anyone walking in on our conversation."

"Makes sense. I had no idea that wharf was in such bad repair."

"Most of it is solid. There are just a few spots. I forgot to watch where I was going." Her mind had been on helping Grace by sharing her own story.

"I'm forever forgetting to watch. I've sprained my ankle more times than I can remember. Did you know that's how I met Greg?"

"No." Peg smiled. Mary was great at stirring a conversation. "Do tell."

Mary put down her needlework, placed a cool cloth on Peg's forehead, and rocked back. "I'd been walking around the pond at the university, and I wasn't watching where I was going.

Apparently, a gopher had burrowed a tunnel across the pathway. I stepped in, fell down, and proceeded to hobble to the school's treatment center. Greg was the student doctor on call."

Peg listened to the older woman ramble on about her husband's exquisite hands and something about his eyes. Peg's own eyes were falling quickly. Soon Mary's words seemed to disappear.

When she opened her eyes, Matt Bower towered over her bed. "Ready for me to take you home?"

thirteen

Peg's complexion had returned to normal. Matt couldn't help but be pleased with her progress. Dr. Hansen had filled him in that morning, letting him know that she'd awoken during the night and that they seemed to be winning the battle over the infection.

"Huh?" Peg blinked her vivid blue eyes.

"I'm here to take you home. Dr. Hansen said you could sleep at home just as easily, perhaps even better, in your own bed." Matt pulled the rocker up beside her bed.

"Where's Daniel?"

"He'll be here shortly. Grace Perez has volunteered to care for you. I'll come by in the evening and report to you the days events at Southern Treasures."

Her gaze darted back and forth. "That isn't necessary, Matt," she whispered.

Yes, it is. "Isn't a problem. I'm happy to help. Your niece, the militant guard—"

"Mariella?"

"Yes, that's the one. . .will also be sleeping in your apartment."

"Daniel can take me home," she insisted.

"He and I just reasoned, and Daniel saw the wisdom in my helping to take you home. If you're uncomfortable with my presence, I understand, and I'm certain we could find another volunteer."

Peg lie motionless before him.

"It's no bother to lend a hand, and my work does not require a nine-to-five work day."

"True."

"Your sister-in-law, Carmen, has the younger children she needs to be fresh for. Grace Perez has no children to watch over. And she seems quite skilled in caring for another in discomfort. I want to help you Peg."

"But what about the rumors?" Peg pulled the covers up to her chin.

"Ahh, well, they already have us married and having children. How much worse can they get? You fell through my dock, Peg. It's the least I could do to help."

Peg mumbled something he couldn't quite make out.

"What?" he asked.

"Nothing. Tell me why you've been working at the store?"

"Well, you've been a tad laid up, wouldn't you say?"

"A simple note on the door would have told folks where I was—not that anyone doesn't know." Peg grinned.

"True, you made the front page of the paper." Matt enjoyed their playful banter. It felt good. It felt healthy. Too many images of Esther being laid up and the pain she suffered had visited his dreams since Peg's accident.

"Tell me it isn't true."

"Afraid it is. You were and still are the big news this week."

"Great," she moaned and closed her eyes.

"Peg, it can't be any worse than the questions I'm being asked all day. For example, 'when are you and Miss Martin getting married?' Or even bolder yet, 'I didn't know you and Peg were already married. How come you didn't invite me to the wedding?' "

Peg's body started to shake with laughter. She grasped her ribs.

"Sorry, didn't mean to make you laugh." Matt held back his own merriment.

"How is the store?"

"Busy. Everyone and their brother has been in to buy just one more item for Christmas. The special orders have been the hardest to track down. Vivian Matlin has been quite helpful on that score. Seems the woman has been in your store a fair amount."

"She has. If it weren't for Vivian, I'm not sure the store would have ever gotten off the ground."

Matt eased back the rocker and crossed his legs at the ankles. "I've kept track of all items sold, and the bank has graciously accepted each day's income to deposit in your account even though I'm not you. I guess the rumors have come in handy also. Or perhaps it's because it's a small secluded place where everyone knows everybody, and they know I'm not trying to set myself up to rob your account. On the other hand, the amount of cash I deposited in the same bank upon my arrival should give me some liberties."

"You've been on this island for such a short time, and you've gotten yourself quite respected. I'm impressed."

"Don't be. It's just the money talking."

Peg knitted her eyebrows. "No, I don't think so. I think it's the man. Folks are seeing you as someone they can trust. Someone they can bank on."

Matt took a deep breath and let it out slowly. *Once she knows the truth of why I've come, she won't be thinking that way.*

"Hi." Daniel beamed as he walked into the room.

Grateful for the distraction, Matt relinquished the rocker and stepped away from Peg's bed.

"Doc says you can come home. Matt borrowed a wagon, and Grace is setting up your apartment. I didn't know you and Grace were such good friends."

"I imagine she feels guilty since she was with me at the time of the accident. But she can use the distraction of helping to take care of me. Not to mention the income. We are paying her, aren't we?"

"If you can get her to take some income, you're a better man than I," Daniel teased. Matt crossed his arms and watched the loving relationship between brother and sister.

Peg grinned. "I'll work on it. So when do I leave?"

"As soon as you're ready to go," Matt responded. "But Doc said he wanted to examine you once more before you leave. I'll be back. Someone asked to pick up an order this morning from your store." Matt waved. "Just have the doctor send someone to fetch me when you're ready."

"Thank you, Matt." Daniel extended his hand.

"Nothing anyone else wouldn't have done. I understand there's been quite a list of volunteers."

Daniel chuckled. "I believe it's given old Doc Hansen the motivation to release her early."

Matt grinned. "You're assumption is probably correct." He left Daniel on the steps of the doctor's house and headed toward the harbor. His grin slipped as the words from Peg echoed in his mind. *Folks are seeing you as someone they can trust.* But he knew the truth: He wasn't worthy of her trust. But could he reveal his secret? Would it be fair? To her? To Micah? To himself?

❧

Peg slid between the covers of her freshly made bed, enjoying the familiarity of the soft feather mattress. Someone had placed poinsettia plants around her room. Their brilliant reds cheered the place.

"Grace, sit down, please. I'm exhausted just watching you."

Grace silently sat beside her on the small oak chair.

Peg felt more like herself every day. Matt's thoughtful attention and ability to make her relax in her own home had been a tremendous help. She also found Grace had been blaming herself for Peg's accident. Over the past few days, Peg had revealed little about her own past, but she thought she had helped Grace understand her own future. Ironically, last night Juan had returned and decided marriage was the answer for him and Grace. Grace, on the other hand, was so nervous she fussed with everything in the house.

"Grace, tell me what you're thinking."

"I don't know, Miss Peg. I want to believe Juan. I know my parents would be much happier when we married. I don't know if I can trust him. Does that make sense?"

"Yes, he ran out on you once. So you're afraid he could do it again."

"*Sí.*"

"Did he explain why he ran?" Peg fluffed up her pillow.

"Something about being afraid."

Peg rolled to her left side. The wounded right leg could easily rest on the lower left one. "Give him a chance, Grace. I'm not saying you should marry him, but if he's serious, he'll wait. He might be able to help you with your own fears. Weren't you afraid when you found out?"

"Terribly."

"But a woman can't run away from it like a man." Peg smiled. "If she runs, the baby comes right along with her."

"*Sí.*" Grace giggled.

"You and Juan are young. You've made some bad choices. That doesn't mean they can't be corrected. We serve a God of forgiveness. He takes our mistakes and fixes them."

"I not so sure about Juan and whether he believes in Jesus."

"Hmm, you might want to ask him." *Juan's lack of faith would definitely be another hardship on this couple, Lord. Give her wisdom,* Peg silently prayed.

Grace fidgeted with a cloth she'd been using as a dust rag.

"What is it?" Peg asked.

"Why are you being so kind to me, knowing. . .knowing. . ." Grace looked down at her feet.

"Because people sin, and I'm no exception. What's the good Lord say about taking that log out of our own eye before we try and take a splinter out of someone else's? We've all made bad choices in our lives, Grace. Thankfully, God's mercy covers them all."

A smile rose on Grace's pink lips. Her dark black hair and dark eyes glimmered with relief. Was it necessary to tell her the rest? That Peg too had been in the same situation at nearly the same age. *No, Grace seems to have gotten the message without the confession.*

"Shall we try and see if I can stand with those crutches?"

"You know the doctor said not for another day."

Peg flopped back down into her pillows. "I feel so helpless."

Grace giggled. "You are."

"I should be working."

"How?"

"I could at least do some embroidery. Surely that isn't going to reopen the wound."

Grace rolled her eyes heavenward. "It's a good thing Mr. Bower is selling everything in your store."

"What? What do you mean?" Peg rose quickly and her sides ached. *Cracked ribs,* she silently reminded herself.

Grace tossed her head from side to side. "Did you hear the word 'selling,' as in, people are buying?"

"Oh."

"You like to control, don't you?" Grace grinned.

"Possibly. I am the older sibling, you know."

Grace wandered off toward the sitting room. Peg hoped

she would bring her needlepoint. Sitting did cause some pressure on her thigh, but she figured if she angled herself just right she might be able to do a couple stitches.

If she were honest with herself, her inability to just lie around was due more to the fact that she missed Matt. She liked Grace, but she felt a constant need to be a mentor for the young woman. Grace was young, while Matt was only a few years older than herself. They even found a few safe things from Savannah to talk about. Peg found herself more and more comfortable with him. She felt a sense of harmony in the house when they were together. And for the first time in more years than she cared to think about, she was considering the possibility of courting. *Courting, at my age. Ridiculous,* she thought.

"Here, Peg. I think you should stay down, though, give that leg some more time to heal," Grace suggested, handing her the needlepoint Peg hadn't touched in nearly a week.

"What smells so good?" Peg hoped Grace would be distracted so she wouldn't see the strain on her face as she shifted her battered body enough to sit up in a reclined position.

"Chicken and dumplings. Cook gave me the recipe."

Peg's mouth watered. If Cook told Grace how to make the dish, it was guaranteed to be good. Peg always liked Cook. Cook was far more vocal then Peg had ever been, but they both loved control and organization. "Smells wonderful."

"Mr. Bower asked for it. Seems he's been missing some of what he calls Southern cooking. Never heard him complain before about the beans and rice, or any of the other dishes I've made."

"I'm surprised he didn't ask for grits."

"Grits?"

"It's a corn dish." How could you describe grits, at least so they sounded edible?

"Never heard of it." Grace sat down beside her and watched Peg weave the needle through the fabric.

"Do you sew?"

"Some, nothing fancy like you."

"Would you like me to show you some stitches?"

"Would you?"

Peg smiled; at last she had found a purpose in being laid up. She'd take on the responsibility of teaching Grace how to do needlework.

❧

"Hello, anyone home?" Matt called as he plopped his attaché on the small table in the sitting room. As much as he hated to admit it, he was behind on some of his own affairs.

Micah had written another letter to confirm his ship and anticipated arrival on Key West. Ten days and his son would be here, the day before Christmas. The question was, would Matt tell him the truth? Would he tell Peg? Every time their discussions revolved around children in general, she was fairly talkative. But once they got to more specifics, to why she never married, she'd claim to be tired and needed to rest. He didn't doubt the need, but it became far too convenient.

"We're in the bedroom, Mr. Bower," Grace called out.

"I'll be right there." Matt pumped some water and washed his hands and face. His nostrils took in the sweet aroma. "Chicken and. . ." He lifted the lid. "Dumplings!" He grabbed a spoon and stirred the pot, sampling a small dose of the broth. His stomach rumbled.

Grace broke out in laughter. "You should see him, Peg. He's like a hungry dog hovering over his dish."

Matt plopped the lid back over the pot. "I was merely sampling your fine cooking."

"Yes, yes. I have to leave for awhile, Mr. Bower. Are you

all set for serving dinner?"

"We'll be fine, Grace. How is she?"

"Getting ready to jump up from that bed and hop around the island."

"I heard that," Peg called out from her room.

Matt smiled at Grace and winked. They both understood just how difficult it was for Peg to be a good patient. To be patient, period. "Thanks for your help." Matt escorted Grace to the front door.

"*Buenos noches*, Peg."

"*Adios, hasta mañana,*" Peg responded.

Matt now understood various greetings and salutations in Spanish. He wasn't certain he'd ever become fluent in the language, especially when he'd heard Peg on more than one occasion rattling off in Spanish to Grace.

"Hungry, Peg?" Matt closed the door behind Grace and walked to the bedroom doorway.

"Starving. I've smelled it cooking all afternoon and not once was I able to steal a taste. I take it Grace caught you scooping out of the pot?"

"Possibly." Matt grinned.

"Well, how was it?" She lifted her body into a sitting position. Her jaw tightened, and her eyelids closed. Pain shouted from her body, but her lips remained silent.

"Wonderful. We'll feast tonight. It's been ages since I've had homemade chicken and dumplings. How about yourself?" Matt stepped back toward the kitchen, lifting a couple of large bowls off a tray Grace had obviously set out earlier.

"Be ready for a real treat. That's Cook's recipe. No one on Key West can cook chicken and dumplings like that woman."

"Cook, Ellis Southard's servant?"

"Housekeeper and cook. Some folks don't like the term

servant when referring to their employees."

"Thanks, I'm still making that adjustment. Please note, I didn't call her a slave. There's something about that woman. I can't picture her ever being anyone's slave."

"Her family was freed when she was a baby. She and her husband George came here from the Bahamas to make a life for themselves."

Matt entered the room with two very full bowls on the tray. "I'm so hungry my stomach is floppin' like a flounder."

Matt chuckled and placed the tray over Peg's lap. "Where'd you get that expression?"

"My father."

"Oh, right, he was a fisherman."

"Yes."

"Do you miss him?"

"Some, but Dan and I have lived apart from them for so many years it's hard to feel the same loss as if I'd seen them everyday."

Matt removed his bowl and sat down in the small oak chair. Definitely a woman's chair. Actually, it felt more like a child's chair. He couldn't picture Peg sitting on it for long periods of time. "Shall we pray?"

They said a brief prayer, then the room silenced. The gentle ting of silver spoons clinking the china bowl lulled him back to Georgia, to Savannah, and to a time when he was a small boy enjoying his first hearty bowl of chicken and dumplings.

"Where were you?" Peg whispered.

"My childhood home, six years old and eating my first bowl of chicken and dumplings. My father loved the meal until he discovered it was common food. It was never served at our table again. Bessy, she was one of our house slaves, would save me a bowl from time to time. And I'd have a real feast. Don't know what it is about this dish, but I sure do love it." He scooped another hearty spoonful.

"Chicken was a treat in our household. We grew up eating tons of fish. Now, don't get me wrong, I enjoy most fish. But when it's your steady diet. . ."

"Say no more, I truly understand."

Peg smiled.

"Do you know you have the most adorable smile. I love it." Matt dropped his spoon in his bowl. Had he really spoken those words? He gave her a sideways glance. Yup, he'd spoken the words. His heart hammered in his chest. He'd been thinking about Peg more and more lately. Not about her injuries, not about her business, and not too much about the fact that she was Micah's mother. But as a woman. Was he really ready to think about another relationship in his life?

fourteen

Peg swallowed the thickest hunk of dumpling imaginable. Had he really commented about her looks? He seemed nervous and as ill prepared as herself. "Matt?"

"I'm sorry, Peg. I didn't mean to be so forward."

"I think we ought to talk about this."

Matt shifted on the chair. Granted, it was a stiff and uncomfortable chair, but that wasn't his problem. "I was merely commenting about your looks. You are a beautiful woman, Peg."

"I see. So the fact that you're squirming like a four-year-old who needs to use the privy has nothing to do with any feelings you might have."

"Are you sure *you* want to discuss this?"

"What is that supposed to mean?" Peg fought to stay still on the bed and not tip the bowl of chicken and dumplings.

He raised his voice slightly. "You're as afraid of your feelings as I am of mine."

Peg silently counted to three before she answered. "What feelings?"

"Try being honest, Peg. You react every time I walk into the room."

If there ever was a problem with pale skin, that was it. The slightest sign of embarrassment and she'd blush brighter than a beacon. Her face flamed. She grasped her spoon. "I'm sorry I brought it up."

Matt nodded and went back to his dinner. The two of them ate in silence until their bowls were finished. "Would you

126

like some more?" he asked.

"No, thank you. I've been sitting for awhile. I should lie down."

He removed the tray and silently slipped into the kitchen. They weren't ready to discuss a relationship. They weren't ready to have a relationship, were they?

"I'm sorry, Peg."

Peg jumped, then groaned.

"Oh, Peg, I'm sorry. I didn't mean to scare you. Are you all right?"

Her leg throbbed. "I'm okay. I'm sorry too."

"I know we both agreed we weren't looking for a relationship, but I think one is developing. I mean, something more than just friendship."

"I know." Peg felt her face brighten yet again.

"I also think we're mature enough to handle this. If the Lord is bringing us together, should we fight it?"

"I don't know, Matt. I don't know that I'd ever be suitable as a wife for anyone."

"What kind of nonsense is that?" His voice raised slightly.

"I'm too old and set in my ways. As Grace put it earlier, I like to be in charge."

"Ah, so submission to a husband is out?"

"Husband? Don't you think you're pushing things?" Peg raised the covers up over her chest.

Matt chuckled. "I wasn't suggesting. I merely was thinking about what you've obviously thought about all these years to remain single."

"Oh. Yes. I guess I decided that would definitely be a hardship on myself and my husband."

Matt sat down beside her on the small chair she used to put on her boots for social occasions. The rest of the time she wore sandals, which she just slipped on.

"Esther had a hard time with that for awhile. She, like you, was the oldest. And the good Lord gave her an incredible brain. Most men would have run away screaming from a woman like that. She said that most men didn't call on her more than once."

Peg laughed. "I think I like your wife."

"Good. You probably would have gotten along really well. But then again, you might have bumped heads too. Hard to say." Matt rose. "I best be going."

"No, Matt. Mariella isn't here."

"I'll go fetch her. Do you need Carmen's help?"

"Yes, thanks."

After Matt returned with Carmen and Mariella and private matters were taken care of, Peg lay down while Carmen changed her dressing. "How's it look?"

Mariella scrunched her nose. "Like fish guts."

"Mariella!" Carmen scolded.

"That bad, huh?" Peg joked back.

Mariella nodded her head up and down and didn't say another word.

"Actually, it's looking much better. The scabs are healing on some of the minor cuts," Carmen offered. "Doc Hansen will be pleased."

"Do you think he'll let me start walking soon?"

"It would be foolish for me to even hazard a guess." Matt said from the doorway.

Carmen looked at Matt, then at Peg. "You two all right?"

"Fine," they both chimed too quickly.

Carmen hid her smile well, but Peg caught a glimpse of it. The leg dressed, Carmen worked on it. Doc Hansen said it would help the blood circulation. What he didn't know was that Matt's gentle and loving ways were dissolving her defenses. If given a chance, she would never mind submitting her authority to this man.

⁊❧

Peg's fondness for Matt was growing day by day. Each day they opened themselves a bit more to each other. Affectionate glances and an occasional caress of each other's hands brought a deeper and deeper intimacy. Conversations about marriage were discussed more freely between them. But if this continued, soon she would have to confess the truth to Matt. It wouldn't be fair for him to enter a relationship with her not knowing the truth. However, finding the right time in which to tell him was hopeless. Their visits were shared with a chaperone. Peg had never been so grateful for the easy distraction of children. She could send them off looking for something, or give them a dollar and ask them to run to town for her. Either way, it provided her only stolen moments alone with Matt.

Peg limped with her crutches to the small sofa. "Mariella went to town for us."

Matt grinned. "Micah arrives tomorrow."

"I can't wait to meet him. The doctor says I can go back to work tomorrow if I'm careful. Mariella said she wouldn't mind spending the day in the store with me."

"Hope you can find everything." Matt winked.

"What have you done?"

He reached out and held her hand. "Peg, we need to talk."

"Peg, are you in there?" Daniel called out, then her front door creaked open.

"So much for a private moment," she mumbled. "Yes," she hollered.

Daniel marched in through the front door.

"What's the matter, Daniel?"

He looked around the room. "Where's Mariella?"

"She ran to town for me." Peg blushed.

Matt released her hand.

Anger rose in Daniel's face.

"Daniel, why were you looking for me?"

"I was going to ask you to help me surprise Carmen for Christmas, but I guess it's a good thing I came in when I did." The anger and disappointment in his voice boomed through the house.

"Daniel." Peg blushed. "You have no right."

"No, Peg. You have no right."

"Daniel," Matt cleared his throat. "Nothing inappropriate has happened. We're both mature adults."

"Nonsense. You know this island and its rumors. Peg's reputation could be soiled. . . ." His words trailed off. He stomped out of the house.

"I'm sorry, Matt. Daniel's right. You should go." Peg rubbed her hands together. Why had she allowed herself to steal private moments with Matt?

"That's ridiculous, Peg. We've done nothing wrong." He stood.

"Please, Matt. You wouldn't understand."

"Try me."

"Please," Peg pleaded. What could she say? This wasn't the way to tell him the truth about herself and her past, something she and Daniel had fought long and hard to protect. Something for which he'd given up his life—to help her rebuild her future. And she had. They had. And in one foolish moment of wanting to be alone with Matthew, she might have ruined twenty years of restoration. How could she have been so foolish?

Matt lifted her chin with his finger and caressed her lips

with his thumb. "Since I've already soiled your pristine reputation, then I guess you won't mind this."

He captured her lips with his. Peg found herself looping her arms around his neck. Her whole world crumbled around her feet as tears ran down her cheek. He released her and boldly stepped away.

"Good day, Miss Martin. If you can't trust me, then we have no relationship."

&

Matt stormed through town. They'd come so close to confessing their love for one another. But how could he truly give her his heart when she hid such a dark secret from him? He couldn't. He wouldn't. It wasn't worth the risk.

He marched to his dock and walked out to the furthest point. Ships sailed gently in and out of the harbor. It had been a mistake to come to Key West. He should have buried the information Dr. Baker had given him so many months ago. Why had he bothered to seek the mother of Micah? To tell her the truth? To tell her that her son did not die?

Her pristine identity in Key West would never welcome the knowledge that her son was alive. Micah would never be accepted. People would always consider him illegitimate. How could a man cope with that information, never having known his entire life that he wasn't his parents' child?

No, it wasn't fair to Micah. He'd been foolish to even think it might be a good thing. Thankfully, Micah knew nothing about Dr. Baker's confession. With everything that was in him, Matt determined he would never tell Micah the truth. He was better off not knowing. While his birth mother had some charming aspects, her heart was hard as stone. She was determined to be something she wasn't, determined to live a life alone. *Well, she can live it alone. I don't need to be here any longer.* It wouldn't be too difficult to move his business back to Savannah. It hadn't really left there yet anyway.

What was he going to do when Micah arrived?

A pelican swooped down in front of him and captured a fish dinner. Matt took in a deep breath and let it out slowly.

A small ship passed and the man at the helm waved. Matt thought he'd met the man before and waved back. Fact was everyone waved as ships passed. A common courtesy of the sea.

A sail—perfect. He and Micah could sail to Key Visca. Spend Christmas together, alone and safe.

Matt headed back from the end of the pier and set about renting a sailboat for the next week.

≈

Peg fought her troubled emotions all night. She had been looking forward to going back to work yesterday. Today the mere thought of it was pure agony. Her leg throbbed. Her concentration was off. The thought of even half a day on crutches made her back stiffen.

She still couldn't figure out why Matt had reacted as he had. Granted, Daniel had too, but that was correctable. Daniel not only apologized, he even went to Matt's home to apologize. Matt had even accepted his apology, but then he said it didn't change the real issue, the real problem.

All night Peg tried to figure out what the "real" problem was. All night she came up blank. She knew she had to tell Matt about her past, but he didn't know that. So she reasoned that couldn't be the problem. But what was their problem? How did he dare say that honesty was the issue? Hadn't she always been honest? Had she ever deceived him about anything?

He never even asked for details concerning her past relationships. He talked freely about himself and Esther, but he never asked about anyone from her past. Why was that?

Daniel knocked on her door bright and early to give her a ride to town. It was hard to believe—she still wasn't strong enough to walk the short distance from her house down to the harbor on her own.

At work, she marveled at the nearly empty shelves. Moving to her new location wouldn't be as difficult as she had anticipated. Matt must be some kind of salesman.

Peg bit her lower lip. Well, that was true. He sold her his heart, and she accepted it. "Why can't we work this out, Lord? I really don't understand the problem."

She rested on the stool and read through all of Matt's entries. He'd been very detailed in every record he kept. She could never question the man's honesty.

"Honesty. Have I been less than honest with him, Lord?" Peg glanced at the harbor. A two-masted schooner was sailing in. She wondered if Micah were on board.

She went back to work, going over Matt's figures. The cries of a ship arriving soon filled the streets. Folks hurried to the harbor in anticipation of packages, guests, and returning family members. Peg looked over the crowd. Matt was nowhere to be found.

The ship slid up along the end of the pier. The seamen jumped on the dock and secured the lines. How many times had she seen ships docking over the years? She couldn't wager a guess. But each time brought her a certain fascination. Most captains were highly skilled, and the ships came to a gentle stop. Once in awhile, you'd get a newer captain, and he'd bang into the pier. Even fewer times she'd seen some damage done to the vessels. But those events were less than a handful.

Today's captain was an expert seaman. His ship kissed the dock with such a tender touch there was hardly a whisper of the lines going taut. Peg smiled.

Soon the passengers started to depart. Some wobbled, but most found their legs quickly. Probably from Savannah, she thought. She watched for Matt's son. One by one, the passengers departed and were greeted by those awaiting their arrivals.

Peg's smile broadened. Nathaniel waved with his arms draped over a young woman. She watched him point toward her window. Peg stood closer and waved in return. Julie must be Mrs. Nathaniel Farris by now. *Won't the island be buzzing?* Peg quickly scanned the locals watching the passengers disembark. Sure enough, women were already smiling and whispering one to another.

Peg chuckled and glanced back at the ship.

A young man with golden waves jumped off the ship. He searched the crowd, looking for his family. Peg took a closer look. Her hands clasped the sill. "Lord, it can't be," she gasped. "Billy."

fifteen

Matt worked his way through the crowd. He'd been late getting up this morning, having spent most of the night packing and making the boat ready for his trip to Key Visca. When word reached his door that a ship was docking, he was only half dressed and hadn't shaved.

"Micah!" he shouted.

His son turned his head toward him. "Excuse me," Matt said stepping past another man.

"Father!" Micah hollered back.

Matt fought the tears that filled his eyes. Both men ran up to each other and wrapped their arms around each other, giving each other a couple of good solid slaps.

"It's good to see you, Son." Matt pulled back and scanned his son from head to toe. Then Matt's stomach flipped. Beyond his son's shoulder, he could see Peg staring at them.

"It's great seeing you. The house is so lonely without you." Micah beamed, then scanned the area.

"I'll be returning with you, I think."

"What? I thought Key West was the answer for the business."

Because your mother is here, and I've fallen in love with her. But he held his inner thoughts at bay. "We'll discuss it later. Where are your bags?"

"A seaman said he'd bring them."

Matt grinned. "I think you're thicker around the middle."

"Too many meals at Anna's restaurant."

"She owns the place?" *Nice change of subject.* Micah's

love life seemed far more appealing to discuss.

"No, she just works there. But she fed me well."

"How's that relationship going?"

"It's not. I mean, I like her and all, but I don't feel the sparks. You know, like you and Mother had."

Matt grinned and fussed with his son's hair. "I know. You'll have to tell me all about her and school. How did your final examinations go?"

"Well, my grades were all in the upper percentiles."

"Wonderful. I knew you could do it, Son. I'm so proud of you."

"Thanks. I had my moments."

Matt chuckled. "Don't we all. Advanced studies can drive a man crazy. Your mother really helped pull me through. She was the distraction I needed."

"Work did that for me. Don't let me forget to tell you about some interesting developments."

"Oh?"

"I may have made some good contacts for us."

"Do tell!"

Micah chuckled. "Later. We have plenty of time."

"True. So how was the voyage?"

"Fine. The weather was calm, no storms." Micah turned his head to the left. Something behind Matt had caught his attention. Silently, Matt prayed it wasn't Peg Martin.

"Hello, Mr. Bower, is this your son?"

Thank You, Lord. "Hello, Ben. Yes. Let me introduce you. Micah, this fine young man is Ben Hunte, and he's very industrious. Ben, this is my son, Micah."

Micah extended his hand. Ben took it, then leaned into Matt and whispered, "Did he own slaves?"

"No, Ben. Micah has never owned a slave."

Ben beamed. "Pleased ta meet ya, Mr. Micah."

"Pleasure meeting you, Ben." Micah caught Matt's eye and raised his eyebrows.

"Later," Matt mouthed.

Micah grinned.

Micah's bags arrived.

"Need help bringing 'em to your house, Mr. Bower?"

"No, thank you, Ben. I think we can handle it."

Ben stepped back. "All right. Have a merry Christmas, if I don't see ya again."

"You too, Ben." Matt reached into his pocket and pulled out a silver dollar. "Merry Christmas."

"Thanks."

"You're welcome. You've been a big help to me while I've been on Key West."

Ben shuffled his feet in the dirt. "I was hoping to get a job from your warehouse, once you built it."

Matt didn't have the heart to tell the child on Christmas Eve that he probably wouldn't be building the warehouse. "We'll see, Son."

Ben ran off after saying good-bye. "What's this about owning slaves?" Micah asked.

❧

Peg grabbed her crutches and headed toward the door. Billy, or rather his look alike, was Micah, Matt's son. Had Esther been a relative of Billy's? Was Matt a cousin of Billy's? Peg couldn't remember Billy ever talking about having rich cousins. He was as poor as her family had been. Which wasn't as poor as some folks, but certainly not as well off as others.

She watched as Ben Hunte had been introduced to Micah. Surely, Matt would bring Micah here. But was that the "truth" that Matt had mentioned yesterday? Did he know she and

Billy had an affair? Could he have just told Matt or his family that he'd had his way with her?

It was all so confusing, and yet it strangely made sense of yesterday's conversation. If Matt had known. . .then he would have known she hadn't told him everything about her past.

Mariella walked into the store. "Is that Mr. Bower's son?"

"I believe so." Peg shifted on her crutches.

"Where's all your stuff?" Mariella demanded with her hands on her hips.

"Appears Mr. Bower's been selling it. And probably told folks to not bring in anything new until after I move."

"Makes sense. Whatcha want me to do?" Mariella scanned the nearly barren room.

"Your father insisted that you come to the store with me. If I didn't expect to hear from him when I returned later in the day, I'd let you go."

"Yes, I hear you. Daniel can be. . ."

"When did you start calling him Daniel?"

"Momma said I don't have to call him Father iffin I don't want to. It's not that I don't love him or nothing. It's just that he isn't my father."

"I understand. I imagine Daniel does too, but don't you think it might be wise to call him, oh, I don't know, something like Uncle Dan, or some other name like Papa, or at the very least, Father Martin or Mr. Daniel?"

Mariella shrugged.

"Showing Daniel respect by giving him the special honor of a special name would make him very proud. I do know he loves you very much."

"Yes, he's a good man, and he's wonderful with my mom. He treats her like she's special. When my father would come home he always made Momma work. Momma said it was the Spanish way. A wife showed honor to her husband by doing everything for him and treating him like a king. Personally, I like Mr. Daniel's way better."

Peg grinned. She turned back to see Micah and Matt heading toward town. Her heart sank that he wasn't bringing his son to meet her. But then again, did she really want to be confronted about her past in front of Mariella or Micah?

No, she would just have to wait until a more appropriate time. After all, Matthew Bower would be staying in Key West for quite awhile. There was plenty of time for them to heal the differences between them. Even if they didn't become anything more than friends, Peg hungered to have their relationship right.

Peg waved as Matt turned back and saw her standing in the doorway.

❧

"Who's that?" Micah asked.

"A friend. Her name is Peg Martin. She and her brother were born in Savannah."

"Really, what happened to her? I mean, why is she on crutches?"

Matt waved back to Peg. As angry as he was with her, he wasn't about to show it in front of his son. Peg nodded and hopped back inside her store.

"She fell through the dock we just purchased."

Micah's jaw dropped. "You bought a rotting dock?"

"In places, yes. It's behind that building she's in."

"That doesn't sound like you, Father. I've never known you to make an unwise business purchase. Is there something between you two that I ought to know about?"

"No. We're friends, nothing more." Matt coughed.

Micah's blue eyes pierced his own.

"Sure."

"Seriously, Son. After her accident I helped her out with her business, and I visited her most evenings."

"You visited her?" Micah turned and headed toward Peg's store. "This woman I've got to meet. Come on, you've got approximately two minutes to tell me everything before I ask the lady myself."

"I owned the dock at the time she had the accident. I felt guilty. After all, I knew the condition of the dock but didn't rope it off, and I didn't put up a No Trespassing sign. Legally, I was responsible for her injuries."

"Now that sounds like my father." Micah grinned. "I still want to meet her. I suspect there might be other emotions at work here besides guilt."

"If there were, and I do mean if, there's no room for anything to develop between us. We look at life differently." A hint of bitterness rolled off his tongue.

"Ouch."

"Micah," Matt groaned.

"All right, all right. You win this time. But trust me, Father, this conversation isn't over. Besides, if you've found someone, I'm sure Mother would be pleased. I know she didn't want you to remain single. She and I talked about it many times before she died."

"You what?" Matt raised his voice. "Why on earth would you and your mother be discussing such matters?"

"I believe she wanted me to be comfortable with the idea if you should ever find someone."

Micah placed his arm around his shoulders. "Your mother was something."

"Yes, she was. I really miss her. With you being gone for the past two months, I've realized just how lonely life is without her and you around."

Matt took a step toward his house, leaving Southern Treasures a step further behind him and Micah. "I rented a boat, Micah. I thought we could sail to Key Visca and have a quiet holiday on the sea."

"I just got off a boat and you want me back on one?"

"I suspect it would be quite conducive for private conversation." Matt leaned closer to his son's ear. "This island has the fastest gossip chain I've ever seen. A lightening strike during dry season hitting the beach grass can't burn faster than this island news. Never seen anything like it before."

"Interesting. I've been hearing a bit more gossip lately from Anna than I ever knew existed between people. That girl can talk. Nothing is safe around her. I learned quickly to guard my tongue. I heard more news about folks I never met than I heard in a lifetime of sitting around talking with my cousins and their servants."

Matt chuckled. "Sounds like she'd love Key West."

"Obviously, we have private matters to discuss, and if an ocean voyage with the two of us is the answer, I'm willing. When do we leave?"

"I hoped tonight, with the evening tide."

"Would the morning one be all right? I'd really like to spend one night in a bed that doesn't move." Micah grinned.

Matt chuckled. "Tomorrow it is then."

"So, where do you live?"

"Couple more houses up on the left." Matt could make out the whitewashed fence in front of the cottage he'd rented. "There," he pointed.

"Not too far from the harbor," Micah commented. "What's all that?"

Matt noticed bundles and packages piled next to his front door. "I have no idea."

る

The sun began to sink in the sky. Mariella turned the OPEN sign in the door window to read CLOSED. "I can't wait to go home."

"Thank you for helping me today. I know we didn't have too many customers, but I'm not as strong as I hoped I'd be."

"I don't mind." Mariella fingered a small stuffed animal. "*Tía* Peg?"

Mariella didn't call her Aunt too often, and rarely in Spanish. "What do you need, Child?"

"I know I said I'd help you but. . ."

"The day is done. It's time to go home and start preparing for our holiday dinner."

"No, I mean, well, I don't want to sound awful, it's just that I have a friend I'd like to give a gift to, but I don't have any money. And I didn't want to ask Daniel, I mean, Papa Dan. . ."

"I like Papa Dan. I think Daniel will like it too."

"Thanks." Mariella looked down at her feet.

"There isn't much left in the store, but pick whatever gift you think would suit your friend. You earned it."

"Really?"

"Yes, Dear. Go ahead." Peg wasn't surprised to see her pick up the small stuffed animal. She'd seen Mariella return to it several times. In fact, Peg had thought she herself might sneak it home as another gift for Mariella. It pleased her to see Mariella picking a gift for a friend instead of something for herself—a definite sign of maturity.

"Thank you, *Tía* Peg."

"Shall we wrap it?"

"You make such pretty packages. It's hard to open them they are so pretty."

Peg smiled and sat on her stool. "Is this friend a boy or a girl?"

"A girl. Her momma works real hard but. . .well, her father also died in the war. They don't have much."

"Hmm, why don't you pick out a couple other things then. Something for her mother. Does she have any brothers or sisters?"

"No, it's just her and her mother. She's only five."

"Would she like one of those dolls over there?" Peg pointed to a couple of rag dolls she still had left.

"Oh, yes." Mariella's face lit up.

"Come on, we have some work to do. Let's put these gifts together as a surprise. If you wish, we could have them delivered to her house, and she wouldn't know who gave them the gifts."

"Is that better?"

"Depends on why you want to give. The Bible talks about us giving to others so that one hand doesn't know what the other is doing. In other words, doing our good deeds in secret. This could be our little secret. Only God will know."

Mariella placed the rag doll and stuffed animal on the counter. "Jesus' birthday is a good time to show people God's love. I think we should do this in secret. Who can we get to deliver our package?"

"I'll find someone. Let's wrap these items up. Under that counter over there I have special squares of fabric just for wrapping gifts. You'll also find some ribbons. Pick some bright reds and greens. Perhaps some ivory too."

Peg gathered a couple items she felt a woman might appreciate and placed them on the counter as well. "Anything else?" she asked Mariella.

"Some of these items you didn't make. You'll have to pay for them."

"True, but I only pay a part of the price. Besides, Mr. Bower made quite a few sales this month. Perhaps I should be laid up more often. I don't think I've ever sold as much merchandise in a month as Mr. Bower sold in the past couple weeks."

Mariella grabbed another small trinket suitable for a child.

"Now let me show you how to wrap this so that it makes unwrapping it just as much fun as receiving the presents."

Her eager student sat down beside her.

The door rattled in its hinges, and they both jumped. Peg looked up at the storefront window and saw Bea Southard frantically waving. "Mariella, open the door for Mrs. Southard."

Mariella obeyed, and Bea pushed into the room. "I'm so glad I caught you. Is it true?"

sixteen

"Is what true?" Peg stood up too quickly on her bad leg.

"That Grace is returning to Cuba with Juan?" Bea sat down at the counter.

"Yes, she told me the other day that she and Juan were going to marry and move to Cuba. He found a job there." Peg looked over to Mariella. She wasn't sure what she knew or didn't know of Grace's condition, and she hoped Bea would catch the movement of her eyes.

"Then I am truly happy for them. What do you have here?"

Mariella chirped, "They are some gifts for a friend of mine."

"They are quite nice. May I help wrap them?" Bea asked.

"Of course. An extra set of hands is always helpful. We're wrapping each item first, then gathering them all together in this cloth."

Bea raised her eyebrows but didn't comment. The three women made short work of it, and Peg gathered the larger cloth around the smaller items and wrapped the edges like a bowl. "Now a delivery man." Peg scanned the street. "Mariella, there's Ben Hunte. Grab him."

Mariella hurried out the front door.

"Okay, what's really the matter, Bea?" Peg quickly asked.

Bea's smile slipped. "Later. Can Mariella go home before you?"

"Yes. I can send her on another errand."

Mariella and Ben returned promptly. "Ben, Mariella knows where this needs to be delivered. We don't want the folks to know where it came from. Just tell them that God loves them."

"I can do that."

Peg reached into her purse and pulled out a silver dollar, handing it to Ben. "Thanks, Ben."

"Nope, it's Christmas. You keep the money. My part of the gift will be the delivery." Ben winked.

"You're growing up too fast, Mister Hunte," Bea praised. Peg placed the coin back in her purse.

A bright white grin appeared on his chestnut brown face. He scooped up the package. "Lead the way, Mariella."

"What's that gift about?" Bea settled on the stool opposite Peg's.

"Mariella has a young friend whose father died in the war. Her mother and she are all alone. I gather they have no other family in the area. I don't know for sure, just my gut instinct. The war's been over for a couple years now. But this young mother appears to have no one else around. Anyway, Mariella kept eying this stuffed animal in the store. Naturally, I thought she liked it and I was going to bring it home for her, in secret, of course." Peg winked. "But it turns out it was for this friend. We just went shopping in the store and gathered a few more items to go with the stuffed animal."

"A few, huh?" Bea chuckled.

"What really brought you in here huffing and puffing?" Peg rubbed her leg.

"Juan and Grace. The way I heard the rumor was that he was forcing her to return to Cuba with him."

Peg laughed and gathered the leftover pieces of fabric and ribbon and put them away under the counter. "This island."

"They were half right. But I wanted to make sure he wasn't forcing her to do anything she didn't want to do."

"Grace is beginning to show. Juan did find a job working

on a tobacco farm in Cuba. If they return to Cuba together, they will face less shame. They married a couple days ago but will be staying through the holiday with her family."

"I'm happy for Grace if this is what she wants."

"She and Juan talked many times. You'd be proud of Grace. She held her own. Juan definitely had to prove his love before she agreed. She didn't want to go to Cuba only to have her husband run off on her again. Her parents gave her a small gift. Juan sees it as a small jewelry case. There's a secret panel in the box that, once removed, reveals some silver and gold coins."

"What?"

"It's for the just-in-case scenario. If Juan should take off on Grace, she has the money to return home to Key West."

"That's not showing much confidence in Juan."

Peg folded her arms around her chest. "It's the money her parents set aside for her wedding. Juan left her once. Grace's father isn't confident the man will stay by her. Personally, I think he will, but her father has a point."

"As a parent, I guess I can understand Grace's father's actions. If I had a daughter I'd want her to be safe."

Peg agreed.

"Is Matt coming to your house for Christmas dinner?"

Peg's heart hammered in her chest. Tears began to pool in her eyes. "No, I don't think I'll be seeing Matthew Bower again. At least, not on a personal level."

"What happened?"

Peg took in short gasps of air. How could she explain? "I think Matt knows about Billy Ingles and our having a baby."

"How? Did you tell him?"

"No, I didn't tell him. Although I was about to. Our relationship was beginning to develop to a point that if we were to go further I would have no choice but to tell him about my past. But just as we were about to share our first kiss, Daniel came storming into the house, saw that the two of us were alone, and hit the ceiling. It was horrible, Bea. I've never seen Daniel behave in such a way before. Granted, I'd never given him the opportunity to be so upset with me. But we're grown adults. Matt and I can have a moment or two alone, can't we?"

"Yes, you can. But I don't understand why that is enough to prevent you and Matt from seeing each other again."

"Micah, Matt's son, is the spitting image of Billy Ingles. I just about fell off my feet when I saw him. Of course, I'm a tad bit unstable on this leg." Peg added, feigning humor.

"How can Matthew Bower's son look like Billy Ingles?"

"He's not an exact copy, and granted I didn't see him up close. He's just familiar enough that I don't doubt that Matt or his wife must have been a relative of Billy's. Somehow Matt must know the truth about my past. And now he doesn't trust me."

❧

Matt fought the need to run, to remove Micah from harm's way all afternoon. The battle waging inside himself was only compounded by the loving gifts that had been brought to his door. Island residents blessed him with home-baked goods for his and Micah's Christmas dinner. He had been given more dinner invitations then he recalled ever having received for all the social occasions he and his wife attended while living in Savannah.

"Reconsidering?" Micah asked, stepping out of the bedroom.

"No, not really. But it will be hard on the folks here when they discover we're not going to move the business to Key West."

"You haven't explained why. What has happened since our last correspondence?"

Micah sat down across from him. His son's blue eyes were so like Peg's. The set of those eyes, and the bridge of his nose. . . Would he ever be able to look at his son and not see Peg Martin, his birth mother? The same woman he had fallen in love with. *God, help me. I can't believe I have such strong feelings for her. If I tell her and Micah. . .* He hesitated. *What would they do?*

"Father?"

"I'm not satisfied with the property. The size of the warehouse I'd be able to build wouldn't suffice. We'd need an additional location, which would mean additional transportation of the goods to and from the harbor."

"But I thought you said you could build upon the present structure."

"True, but I've been reconsidering."

"Would you mind terribly showing me the property? Perhaps I could come up with an alternative. That isn't to say I don't think you've explored all the options but. . ."

"No, I don't mind." Matt pulled out his pocket watch. Peg would have left the store hours ago. It was safe to go there. "Why don't we go now before the sun sets?"

Micah gave him a lopsided grin. "Sounds good."

The two of them headed toward the harbor, back toward Southern Treasures. The sign on the door said CLOSED. Matt breathed a sign of relief.

Micah placed an arm across his father's shoulder. "Is she someone I should meet?"

Matt blinked back the honest question from his son. Yes, he should. But if he did, their lives would be forever altered. "I think it's best that we not pursue a relationship."

"So, you *did* find someone?" Micah grinned. "Mother would be pleased, you know."

"What?" Matt walked around to the backside of Peg's store. The fresh boards reminded him of the horrid scene when he came upon seeing Peg twisted between the rotting boards.

"Look, I'm not the one to give you advice about love and relationships. I'm still learning that for myself. But like I said, Mother and I spoke on the matter before she died. We both agreed a good wife would be best for you."

"You two decided, huh?" Matt teased.

"Come on, Father, you like her, don't you?"

"Yes, I like her. But we come from different backgrounds. Our values are not the same."

"She's not a believer?"

"No, she's a believer. Has a healthy relationship with the Lord. It's not that." How much longer could he skirt around the real issue?

"Anna isn't a believer, which is one of the reasons I know she's not the right one for me. At first I wondered if God would use our friendship to help bring her to salvation. I still hope He might. But I know it's wrong to set one's heart on an unbeliever. So I kept my guard up. Slowly, I began to see that, while we had some similar interests, we looked at life totally differently. In a way, she thinks the world owes her something, I guess because her father was hung for murder when she was a tiny baby. She doesn't see a need to give something back to society."

"Ah, I've met a few of those in my lifetime. It's one of the things we need to guard ourselves against with our employees. Some feel they don't need to work for their wages. Just their showing up should be enough."

Micah chuckled. "You wouldn't believe how many assumed, because you were gone, that I would be an easy touch. You've taught me well, Father. Hard work is to be rewarded. Sloths can find the door."

Matt grinned. "I'm proud of you, Son. But tell me, is this what you want to do with your life? Peg made me realize that I'd done the same with you as my father had done with me. I've assumed you would want to take over the business one day. You don't have to; the choice is yours. You can use your education and pursue any career you'd like."

"Now I'm definitely going to have to meet this Peg Martin."

Matt's stomach tightened.

"What's the matter, Father? What happened between the two of you?

seventeen

Matt sat down on the end of the dock and patted the board beside him. Taking in a deep breath he let it out slowly. "Micah, I have something to tell you. But before you hear it, I need to hear you say that you know that I love you."

"Father, I know you love me. I've never doubted that love for a moment."

"Good, because what I'm about to tell you will shake the very foundations of that love."

"What?"

"Bear with me, Son. This is difficult."

Micah nodded and clenched the end of the dock, rocking slightly.

"About three months ago, I was called to a man's bedside because he was dying, and he felt he needed to tell me something about his past."

Micah nodded, his face sharp with interest.

"His name was Doctor Baker."

"Our old doctor?"

Micah gave a single nod. "Doc Baker said he needed to tell me something. I had no idea what it was. I thought a pastor would be the more appropriate person, but a man doesn't turn aside a dying man's request."

Micah's golden brown eyebrows knitted.

Matt took in another deep breath and eased it out slowly. *Oh, Lord, help me do this right,* he silently prayed. "He told me that he had taken a newborn baby from a young mother and replaced it with an infant that had died during childbirth."

"What? Who did he think he was, God?"

"Apparently. He reasoned that this young mother, who wasn't married, wouldn't be able to raise the child. And the couple whose child had died would be good parents."

"But that's unethical." Micah's sense of justice and the idealism of youth brought out his zeal for what was right.

"Exactly."

"Why was he telling you this? Why are you telling me?"

Matt paused. "Because, Micah, my dear, dear son—" Matt choked back the tears.

"No!" Micah blurted. "No, Father. It can't be true. I'm your son."

"Yes, you are my son. Nothing will ever change that." Tears streamed down Matt's face. "I love you. You're as much a part of me as life itself. I didn't want to believe it, either. But as some time passed, I started putting some things together."

"Such as?" Micah's knuckles were white from holding the deck so tightly.

"You're hair and skin coloring. No one in my family or your mother's has blond hair."

"But. . ." Micah's eyes brimmed with tears.

"It doesn't change the fact that I love you, Micah. I loved you as my son and you are my son. I've raised you. You're a part of me and your mother. Nothing will ever change that."

"Did he tell you who I really am?" Micah looked out at the sea.

"Yes," Matt whispered.

"And?" Micah demanded.

"I don't know who your father is, but he gave me the name of the girl who gave birth to you."

"And?" Micah raised his voice, his gaze now firmly planted on Matt's own.

Please, Lord, help him understand. "She moved away from Savannah twenty years ago."

"Who is she? Where is she?"

"I tracked her down, Micah." Matt paused. "I'm so sorry, Son. I thought of not telling you. But I honestly don't know that I could keep it in much longer. The fact is, the girl who gave birth to you lives on Key West."

"That's why you came here? Why didn't you tell me? Why all this secretiveness? We've never kept secrets before. Not about Mother dying—nothing, ever. Why now, Dad?" Micah stood up and paced back and forth on the dock.

"Because I needed to find her. I needed to find out whether I should tell you or not. I wished Doctor Baker had taken his unethical practice to the grave. Our lives were better off not knowing."

"And what of this woman who is my mother? What of her life, Dad? Was it right for her to believe her child was dead all these years? Was it?" Micah's voice mirrored the red fire of the sunset.

"No, Son. It wasn't fair." Matt hung his head. The truth of the matter was out. It wasn't fair. It wasn't fair to anyone.

"Does she know? I mean, did you tell her?"

"No."

Micah stomped further away down the dock. Then stopped and faced him. "You're as bad as Doctor Baker was. Who is she, Dad? Who is my mother?"

❧

Peg finished dressing her presents for Daniel and his family. She set aside the two items she had purchased for Matt and Micah. He wouldn't be coming to Christmas dinner; she could feel it in her bones. He hadn't introduced his son to her.

The memory of his kiss still burned her lips. Peg closed her eyes and quelled her emotions. She wouldn't dwell again on that kiss. When she opened her eyes, the gifts blinked like the twinkle of moonlight dancing on an ocean. She would take them to his doorstep and leave them there. No, she corrected herself, she wouldn't take them. She'd have Daniel do it. She didn't need to see Matt. She just wanted to. But how would she explain her past? A past he obviously knew about? He must think her dishonest.

But why should the entire world know her sin? Peg paced back and forth in her apartment until her leg throbbed. She sat down and raised her leg, massaging it as the doctor had taught her. The wound was healing well, though it looked uglier than sin. Peg caught herself in her thoughts. Sin. . . ugly. . . She closed her eyes and blinked back the tears. Her own sin had scarred her heart as badly as the beam puncturing her thigh. But God's grace covered that sin with the shed blood of the cross. The scar remained; the sin did not.

She knocked on the door joining her apartment to the big house. No one answered. She turned the handle and entered. The kitchen was hot, and the fragrance of fresh baked breads and pastry filled the air. "Hello, anyone home?" she called.

"*Tía* Peg." Mariella came running. "I hid in the bushes. I saw Lisa and her mother find the package on their front step. Ben placed the bundle on the step, rapped the door, then ran, hiding around the corner of the house. Oh, *Tía,* they cried. It was so beautiful."

Peg reached over and embraced her niece. "Yes, it is wonderful to give to others and not expect a reward."

"Yes. Thank you. I would never have been able to give them such fine presents."

"Remember, it wasn't us. It was God working through us. We just happened to be in the right place at the right time."

Mariella nodded in agreement.

"But it still feels good, doesn't it?" Peg encouraged.

"Yes," Mariella beamed.

"Where's Papa Dan?"

"Upstairs with Momma."

Peg listened. Hearing no sounds, she decided not to interrupt them. They were probably taking care of last-minute details for the Christmas holiday. "Would you tell him, when he has a free moment, I need him to run an errand?"

"Sure. Can I do it for you?"

"No, thank you. The sun is set. I think Daniel should be the one to deliver it for me."

"You're right, Papa Dan doesn't want us in town when the sun goes down."

"Wise man, your Papa Dan." Peg smiled. Daniel had been truly blessed with quite a family.

Back in her own apartment, she pulled out some needlework and tried to get back to the calm she'd known before Matthew Bower had come to Key West.

*

Hours later, Peg found herself alone yet again. Daniel had come and gone. She had enjoyed a meal with his family. Now she faced the empty sounds of a house devoid of hope and love. How she appreciated and missed Matt's presence. Their time together. Their playful banter. Her stomach tightened, and she massaged her throbbing leg.

A sudden knock on her door startled her. "Who is it?" she called out.

"Matt. Peg, open up, please."

Peg worked her way to the door, using furniture for crutches.

She found Matt with his hair disheveled, his eyes red. He appeared to have aged ten years since she last saw him. "What's the matter?"

"Is Micah here?" He looked past her into the sitting room.

"No, why would he be? What's wrong, Matt?" Peg fought the desire to reach out and touch him. She remembered all too well his reaction when she'd done that in the past.

"We need to talk." He walked past her and made himself comfortable on her divan. "Come join me, Peg."

She hobbled over to the sofa and sat beside him. "All right, Matthew, what is the problem? Has something happened between you and your son?"

"Yes. No. I don't know. Look, I came to Key West for a reason. I don't know how to say it other than to say it straight out." Matt raked his black hair back with his right hand.

"All right." Peg sucked in a deep breath. He was going to tell her he knew the truth. Her hands trembled. She held them on her lap.

"I came to Key West because of a dying man's confession. This man had done something so unthinkable I had prayed it wasn't true. But now, in the end, I know it is true. I even, at one small moment, hoped and prayed his confession was the result of the disease that was taking his life. But it wasn't. Peg, that man was Doctor Baker. I think you knew him too."

Peg gasped. "I'm sorry, Matt. I would have told you the truth of my past and why I came to Key West if our relationship developed any further. In fact, I was about to tell you that same day of our argument. I didn't know you knew."

"Peg." Matt grasped her hand. "I know. But it's not what you think I know."

"What?" Peg searched his dark green eyes.

"Hear me out, please," he pleaded.

Peg nodded.

"Doc Baker confessed to me that he switched a young woman's baby with another baby. They were both born minutes apart from each other. He delivered them both."

Peg knit her eyebrows in confusion.

"Peg, he switched your son with my dead son."

"What?"

"Micah is your son."

A sob groaned out of her throat, a fury of emotions and no discernible thought. What could she think? Her baby was dead. No, Matt said his son was her son? "But how? Why?" Tears burned a track down her cheek.

"I don't know. He knew my wife could never have another child after she gave birth. He also knew you weren't married. I guess he assumed—"

Peg jumped up and screamed.

Matt leapt to his feet and held her. "Is it your leg?"

"Yes. No. Let go of me!" She pushed him away. "You've known this since you arrived on Key West and you didn't tell me? Were you planning on not telling me the truth? Why did you come looking for me? So you could shame me?"

Daniel came running into the apartment. "What's going on in here?"

"Matt says John isn't dead. That his son, Micah, is my son."

"What?" Daniel stood toe to toe with Matt. "Are you daft?"

"Doc Baker confessed he switched our babies."

"What?" Daniel plopped down onto the sofa. "This is ridiculous. Doctors don't do that."

"Apparently, Doc Baker thought he had the perfect solution," Matt groaned. "I can't deny that I am glad he switched the babies. I love Micah. He's such a part of me and my wife. I never would have thought in a million years that he wasn't my son. But he is my son. I've raised him."

"So, where does that leave me?" Peg cried. "I've mourned the death of my baby for twenty years. I've stayed away from relationships bound and determined that God kept me single because of my past. And that still may be the case. But I have a son, a son who's alive and breathing, who doesn't know me."

Peg collapsed on the rocking chair. "When I saw Micah get off the ship I nearly fainted. He's the spitting image of Billy."

"Not really. I never met Billy, but I know my son, and he has your eyes, and your hair coloring, although his hair is wavy."

Peg held her sides and rocked. *My son is alive? My son is Matt's son, Micah.*

"Peg?" Matt knelt in front of her. "I'm sorry. I should have told you sooner but—"

"But you couldn't decide if I was worthy," Peg fired back. "Get out of my house, Matt. I need to be alone."

"Peg, please. I need your help. We need to find Micah. He's been gone for hours. He wasn't pleased with me, either."

Daniel got up. "He looks like Billy?"

Peg nodded.

"I'll go find him. Just let me tell Carmen first."

"Thank you," Matt offered. "With all of us looking, we should be able to find him."

"To think I almost gave my heart to you," Peg hissed. "I can't believe you would keep something so important from me."

"Peg, try and understand. I had to think of Micah too. What's it going to be like for him to learn the truth? Would it be fair to him to have him labeled as illegitimate? I thought Key West might provide the place for him to live with no shame, but this place is so gossip infected no one could have a chance here."

"Well, we may have a problem with gossip, but we're island folk, and island folk stick together. I'm not saying it wouldn't have been rough for awhile. Goodness, no one here even knows about my past. Well, except Daniel and Bea Southard. No one would believe it. But then they would remember who I am. They know me, they trust me. They'd understand, in time. At least my friends would."

"I'm sorry. You're probably right. But it's just as much of a shock for me as it was for you. I never would have thought my son wasn't my son. Just saying it doesn't make it seem plausible."

As much as she wanted to be angry with Matt, he did make sense in a strange sort of way. He did love his son. He couldn't stop talking about his son. To all of a sudden find out Micah wasn't his biological son must have sent the man spinning like an eddy during the change of tides.

"We'd best get started," Peg decided and grabbed her crutches. She couldn't go far, but she'd go as far as her legs would allow.

"I'll go to town and check out the taverns," Matt replied. "Micah isn't a drinker, but this kind of news could cause the strongest of men to drink."

"I'll check the waterfront," Daniel volunteered.

"I'll work my way through the streets closer to this side of the island."

With great effort, Peg limped her way through the various streets between her home and Matt's cottage. Minute by minute, hour by hour, her leg throbbed. She needed to take a break. Her heart ached. Her mind was confused; she was a mixture of emotions—anger toward Doctor Baker, resentment at Matt for keeping this information to himself. In some small way, she understood his confusion. But it didn't dull her anger. Or, as she thought about it, perhaps it did. A little.

The same judgmental attitude that Doc Baker showed was the very reason she had moved to Key West to start fresh. Now she discovered the pain and agony of losing her child had been false. Her son wasn't dead. He was alive, alive and well. But he belonged to another. She would never know what it was to watch him grow up. To see him take his first steps, speak his first words. Nothing. All of it snatched away because of some self-righteous old man. Peg's nostrils flared.

She rarely got this angry. She needed to calm down. She worked her way down a street that ended at a small inlet. Her mourning place. The small stretch of beach where she sought God out year after year to try to understand why things had happened as they had.

She needed to rest. Peg sat down on a fallen palm tree and rubbed her leg. The moonlight glistened on the water. "Father, comfort Micah."

The long leaves of a nearby bush rattled in the wind. Peg glanced over to see a man stand up and march over toward her.

"You're my mother, aren't you?"

eighteen

Matt was frantic. Hours of searching and nothing. Not only could he not find Micah, he'd lost track of Peg as well. Daniel had returned home unable to find Micah at the waterfront. The two men decided that time was what Micah needed. So Matt wandered down another street looking for Peg. She couldn't have gone too far on those crutches. But then again, he couldn't imagine what was going on in her mind at the moment.

Matt rubbed the back of his neck. Time was what everyone needed. Time to heal and time to understand just what had happened to all of them because of one man's tragic lack of judgment.

Coming to a dead end, Matt turned around and retraced his steps. He plunged farther back from the harbor trying to find Peg. He needed to talk with her. No, he *wanted* to talk with her. To try to explain his heart.

Peg had to be somewhere. He pushed his way up another narrow street. The darkness of night, the covering of the trees, brought out the fear he'd buried deep inside. *Lord, let her be all right.*

Several times he'd backtracked to her apartment. He'd even gone back to his own. She was still out there, somewhere. *Where could she be, Lord?*

&

"Yes, Micah. I guess I am."

Micah sat down beside her. She silently thanked the Lord for a full moon, so she could see his face. She reached out to touch him. He didn't pull away. Her fingers shook as they caressed her son's features. "You look a lot like your father."

"Who is he?"

Peg turned away from her son. She had to confess the truth. He of all people deserved to know the truth. She swallowed hard. "At the time, I loved him very much. We were going to get married. At least that's what I thought. Turns out it was just another case of Billy's smooth tongue. My brother Daniel tried to warn me. But he was several years younger, and I thought I knew it all."

"Tell me, tell me everything," Micah pleaded.

"Oh, Micah, I've mourned you terribly." Peg wiped a tear from her face. "I was just about eighteen when I met Billy. He seemed so exciting. So unlike the other boys in town. He didn't work on the fishing boats, and he didn't smell like fish." Peg paused. "At the time, that was quite an advantage."

Micah chuckled.

"Anyway, he was a bit wild, and I was a bit rebellious. I fell madly in love with him, or rather, with the idea of being wild and free. I overlooked Billy's bad habits, his ability to have money without working hard. That should have put up a warning flag, but it didn't. Anyway, he promised we'd get married when I was eighteen. I turned eighteen and found out I was expecting you. I was scared at first, but then I thought how wonderful to have a product of our love growing inside of me.

"Billy didn't see it that way. He thought it was all my fault and said he wasn't raising no brat. He left, and I had to go home and tell my parents the truth. They sent me away to have the baby. But as the time to deliver came close, my mother wanted me near her. So I lived the last days of my pregnancy at a rooming house near Doctor Baker's office." She sighed.

"The rest I figure you've heard from your father."

"He's not my father."

Peg reached out and held his hand. Micah wrapped his fingers around hers. "Oh, Micah. He is your father. Billy Ingles would have ruined your life."

"Billy Ingles is my father?" Micah's voice was high with disbelief.

How does he know Billy? "Yes, do you know him?"

"No, not really. I met his daughter. Oh, no!" Micah grabbed his stomach.

"Are you all right?" Peg draped her arm over his shoulder.

"I met his daughter, Anna Ingles."

Billy had another child? Peg calmed herself by taking in a deep breath.

"I almost courted her. Can you imagine? My own sister?"

If Peg ever wanted to curse someone right now, it was Doctor Baker. "No, I can't imagine. I'm sorry, Micah. It's all my fault."

"All your fault? Dad said Doc Baker did this."

"True, but if I hadn't sinned with Billy, none of this would have happened."

"But then I never would have existed." Micah reached down and picked up a handful of sand and let it run through his fingers. "How long have you been here?"

"I moved to Key West with my brother Daniel shortly after we buried the baby."

"It's a good thing Doc Baker isn't alive. I'd have a mind to—"

"Micah, your parents didn't raise you to behave that way," Peg scolded.

"I know. I'm just so angry. It's horribly unfair. I don't know what to feel. I think of the word mother, and I think of my mother. Now, I look at you and see I am a part of you. I just don't know what to think."

"Why don't we just take it one step at a time? Matt and Esther were your parents. They raised you. They went through every sleepless night a parent goes through for a child. I, on the other hand, mourned a child I never knew. I want to get to know you, Micah. But you're not a child; you're a man. The most we could ever hope to have is a close friendship, one adult to another."

"I suppose you're right. I can't separate who I am from who I was supposed to be."

Peg grinned. "God says if we wait on Him, He'll make our paths straight. This is one of those times when the paths are not very straight, where people have gotten in and messed with God's plan. I messed with it by getting involved with Billy in an inappropriate way. Doc Baker messed with it by trying to correct a wrong. Somehow, I know if we give God enough time, He will work this all out."

"Tell me about yourself," Micah pleaded. "I want to know you."

"Only if you tell me all about yourself." Could it be this easy? Could they become friends? She looked at Micah and saw herself and Billy. Always Billy. He would permanently be a part of her past, a part she'd blocked out for many years. She waited for Micah's response.

"Fair enough. You start."

"All right, my name is Margaret Elizabeth Martin, but everyone calls me Peg. My father was a fisherman. . . ."

ᴥ

Matt listened in the distance. He'd come upon Peg sitting on the log when he heard Micah approach her. They were talking. His first instinct, to come to Key West and correct a wrong, had been correct. He had lost his son, but it was the right thing in the end.

Matt walked back toward the cottage, leaving mother and son to their discovery. They needed time. He grabbed his duffel bag and loaded up some provisions for his sail. His trip was in order as well. It would give Peg and Micah a chance to get to know one another. Maybe someday they would forgive him for his deceit.

With the boat loaded, he trekked back to the cottage and penned a letter to Micah.

Dear Son,
   I've decided to take that trip and give all of us a
chance to calm down. Peg Martin is a wonderful woman.
You were correct when you sensed we had feelings for
one another. But the past will probably prevent us from
having a future. I'll return in a few days and we can talk.
   Know this one thing, Son. I love you. I always have,
and I always will.

                                        Your father forever

Matt swallowed hard. He'd done enough crying for a grown man in two lifetimes. He'd always seen himself as a strong man, but Esther's death, Doc Baker's deception, and the loss of his son were more than one man should be asked to bear in his lifetime.

He closed the door to the cottage as a predawn glow gave a surreal feel to the day. The yellow and white light dancing on the waves cast an orange tone to his skin. Palm trees were dark silhouettes against the eastern sky.

"'Mornin', Mr. Bower. Heard your son came in yesterday." A local fisherman stepped from his boat to the dock with such an easy stride anyone observing would know he'd grown up along the water.

"Yes, Sir." What else could he say? It was Micah and Peg's choice to reveal the truth of their relationship, not his.

"Where ya headin'?"

"Key Visca. Thought a short sail would be nice."

"Just the two of you, or are you bringin' Miss Martin along?"

Matt groaned.

"Sorry, didn't mean nothin'. Just heard you two were getting married."

Matt pulled the line to bring the boat closer to the dock. "We're just friends." He almost threw in they had never even kissed, but then he remembered his actions in Peg's home the other day.

"Sorry, guess a man ought to ask before he assumes. Have a good sail. Wind's coming up from the southwest, should have a nice tropical breeze pushing up the coast."

"Thanks." Matt waved as the man boarded his boat. He cast off the bowline and gave the vessel a slight push away from the dock as the fisherman stepped on board. Odd, Matt thought, that he was going out on Christmas morning.

Matt boarded his sailboat, made the mainsail ready, and went below to retrieve the jib. In the ship's hold, he rummaged through the bow looking for the right sack that contained the jib. Finally he spotted it and neatly placed everything that wasn't needed back into the bow.

As he poked his head out of the hold, Peg stood before him with her hands on her hips. Her crutches lay on the dock. "And just where do you think you're going?"

&a

Peg braced herself. The leap to the boat had put a lot of strain on her leg.

"Key Visca." Matt pushed past her.

"And for what purpose?"

"Peg, you and Micah deserve time to get to know one another. I need to give you and him time to absorb the full ramifications of what has happened."

Peg struggled to grasp something as her leg lost its strength. Matt caught her in his arms and lifted her up off her feet. "Sit down before you damage that leg some more. It's swollen, Peg. You've been on it too long."

"I know." Peg smiled as Matt worked his hands down her leg.

"Lie down and lift your leg," Matt ordered. "Have you been up all night?"

"Yes. Same as you; same as Micah. Matt, don't go. We need to talk." Peg reached out and placed her hand on his shoulder.

"What is there to talk about? Doc Baker took Micah away from you."

She could feel his body tense below her fingers. "Yes, but. . ."

"No buts, Peg. It was wrong. You know it. I know it. Micah knows it. And before too long, everyone will know it."

Peg looked along the shore. No one was in sight. Due to the Christmas holiday, most folks were still snug in their beds. "Probably. I can't hide the truth any longer. But, Matt, I want you to hear from me what happened, who Micah's father is, why a foolish girl of seventeen—nearly eighteen found herself in such a predicament."

"I think I understand the process, Peg. Where's Micah?"

"At the house. I told him I would stop you from setting sail if you hadn't already left. He's lying down. It was quite a shock for him."

Matt frowned and looked out to sea.

"Matt, please. I think you and I. . .well, I think we started to have rather strong feelings for one another, but we're both too scared to admit it. I've got nothing to hide now. You know everything about me. Well, almost everything. Am I such a terrible person that you wouldn't want to have a relationship with me?"

"Goodness no, Peg. I enjoy talking with you, spending time with you. I knew from the first moment I stepped on the island who you were. But that didn't stop me from—"

"From what, Matt? Say it."

"From falling in love with you," Matt whispered. He knelt down beside the seat where she was lying down with her leg propped up on the outer rail.

"Oh, Matt. I love you too. I've fought it, but when you kissed me I couldn't deny it any longer."

"What about the past? What about Esther and me raising your son?"

"Our son. You and Esther will always be his parents. The best I can hope for is a close adult relationship with Micah. Maybe, in time, a special bond. I love him with all the passion I felt for my child when I thought he was dead. But it doesn't erase the fact that I had no hand in raising him. He's a lot like me, you know."

"Yes, I know," Matt grinned.

"Oh, I suppose you do."

"How's Micah with all of this?" Matt asked.

"Wondering when you're going to be a man and kiss the woman," Micah piped in from the dock.

"Micah," Matt and Peg called out. There he stood, with his arms crossed over his chest and a foolish grin on his face. The past hours had not been wasted. Peg had been able to share some of a parent's heart with Micah, helping him understand Matt's actions, and convincing herself in the process of why Matt had done what he had. Why he had kept the secret so long.

"Well, are you going to kiss this woman and begin our new lives?" Micah demanded.

"Hmm." Matt wiggled his eyebrows.

Peg giggled.

"Should we seal our future with a kiss, Miss Martin?" Matt brushed the top of her lips ever so lightly with his finger.

Peg groaned and felt her face flush.

"Micah, would you please turn around?" Matt motioned with his finger.

"Father, you can't be serious," he said, but he obeyed his father.

"Now, where was I?"

Peg felt her face grow hotter still.

"May I?" he whispered.

She blinked her agreement and relished the sweet surrender of their lips connecting, of becoming vulnerable one to the other. Her life verse flooded back in her mind, Isaiah 40:31: *But they that wait upon the Lord shall renew their strength; they shall mount up with wings as eagles; they shall run, and not be weary; and they shall walk, and not faint.*

God had turned her painful mistake into a long-awaited blessing.

Micah coughed, then tapped his foot loudly. "Folks are gathering, you two."

Matt pulled away. Peg tried to draw him back. His finger touched her lip. "Not now, my sweet, my southern treasure. What a wonderful Christmas gift you are. Merry Christmas, Peg."

"Merry Christmas, Matt." She smiled, her heart spilling over with joy. God had given her a special gift this year—a new family of her very own.

A Letter To Our Readers

Dear Reader:

In order that we might better contribute to your reading enjoyment, we would appreciate your taking a few minutes to respond to the following questions. We welcome your comments and read each form and letter we receive. When completed, please return to the following:

Rebecca Germany, Fiction Editor
Heartsong Presents
PO Box 719
Uhrichsville, Ohio 44683

1. Did you enjoy reading *Southern Treasures* by Lynn A. Coleman?
   - ❑ Very much! I would like to see more books by this author!
   - ❑ Moderately. I would have enjoyed it more if

   _____

   _____

2. Are you a member of **Heartsong Presents**? Yes ❑ No ❑
   If no, where did you purchase this book?_____

   _____

3. How would you rate, on a scale from 1 (poor) to 5 (superior), the cover design?_____

4. On a scale from 1 (poor) to 10 (superior), please rate the following elements.

   _____ Heroine   _____ Plot

   _____ Hero   _____ Inspirational theme

   _____ Setting   _____ Secondary characters

5. These characters were special because _____
   _____
   _____

6. How has this book inspired your life? _____
   _____
   _____

7. What settings would you like to see covered in future
   Heartsong Presents books?_____
   _____
   _____

8. What are some inspirational themes you would like to see
   treated in future books?_____
   _____
   _____

9. Would you be interested in reading other **Heartsong
   Presents** titles?   Yes ❑   No ❑

10. Please check your age range:
    ❑ Under 18   ❑ 18-24   ❑ 25-34
    ❑ 35-45   ❑ 46-55   ❑ Over 55

Name _____

Occupation _____

Address _____

City _____ State _____ Zip _____

Email _____

NEW ENGLAND

From the majestic mountains to the glorious seashore, experience the beauty New England offers the romantic heart. Four respected authors will take you on an unforgettable trip with true-to-life characters.

Here's your ticket for a refreshing escape to the Northeast. Enjoy the view as God works His will in the lives of those who put their trust in Him.

paperback, 476 pages, 5 ⁹⁄₁₆" x 8"